The I

By Melanie Ross

The Hope Chest Story by Melanie Ross
Illustrations by Tess Hiembach

First Printing June 2012

Copyright © 2012 Underwood Publishing

Printed in the USA

Catalogued with the Library of Congress 2012

ISBN 9780-6156-2337-5

Underwood Publishing
7290 Navajo Road
San Diego, CA 92119

www.UnderwoodPublishing.com

Underwood
Publishing

This book is dedicated to my mother Minnie
who always believed in me and loved this story
from the first draft. She recently passed away
but I'm sure she is smiling down now
on the finished book!

This book is also dedicated to my children
Cameron & Madeline
who were my first and incredibly enthusiastic fans.
They begged me to read the book over and
over in my theatrical Irish accent during
our bedtime reading marathons!

And to my husband Mark who
truly loved my book from the getgo,
and who believed in me and said,
"this must get published, its wonderful!"
So, of course, he made it happen!

Chapter 1

A green fog entered the Godforsaken cave deep in the forest. The mist seemed alive as it made a humming noise and slowly but surely, wound its way through the cave like a hovering fat snake chasing away the clear cold air. It was so thick that you couldn't see your own hand in front of your face. Strange gurgling laughter, evil and hideous to listen to, permeated the cold green air. The fog made its way toward the laughter as a child runs to its mother. The sound was unlike any earthly animal or human. Goosebumps accompanied the overwhelming fear it caused and the sticky emerald green fog made them worse. Muffled sounds, as though someone was pounding, could be heard and slowly faded away to silence....

Bridget's head was deep inside as she inhaled the scent

of the old musty cedar chest, "Mmmmmm." Suddenly she was yanked up abruptly.

"Bridget, what do you think you are doing?! This old chest lid could have fallen on top of you and broken your neck!" Bridget's mom scolded as she straightened her daughter.

"But Mom, I can't understand the soul of this old chest if I don't smell where it came from."

Bridget's mom laughed and found herself listening to her words coming back to her. Candace smiled at her skinny daughter who was almost as tall as her five-foot-four inch frame. Bridget had long, blonde, silky, straight hair that she usually wore in a high pony-tail that swung constantly with her every move. She wore wire-framed glasses that sparkled with glitter when you looked closely at the skinny wires.

The subtle sparkle emphasized her dancing blue eyes that were full of expression. Her tanned skin was almost always clad in flowery bike shorts with t-shirts and socks to match. She liked being a girl but shorts were her favorite so she could 'quick get on my bike' as she always remarked; and secondly, 'of course the boys couldn't accidentally see my underwear if I'm climbing'. For her twelve years, she was as practical as an adult and always thought of every possible consequence. Her long ponytail was always swinging around from Bridget's non-stop activity. When the ponytail was perfectly still you could tell Bridget was reading or sleeping.

Candace O'Riley watched her daughter gently run her hands over the polished wood of the chest. Then Bridget looked up at her mom longingly.

"Please mom, can I have it?"

Candace winced inside with pain. She could see that her daughter's love of antiques was deep. She often joked with her husband that Bridget was a reincarnated antique dealer. But, unpleasantly, she couldn't afford it.

"Bridget I can't, we don't have the money, I'm sorry. We need to go. I have to make dinner." She took her daughter's hand and firmly led her out of the antique store. It was she who had taught her young daughter to love antiques.

"The character and soul of antiques makes them special. Age means everything with old furniture." Bridget parroted her mother as they got back in the car. Candace quietly resolved to find a way to teach Bridget that the souls of people were more important. Little did she realize that her daughter already knew that. Bridget, fidgeting in the back seat, wished her best friend Esther was there. They both believed highly in intuition and the spirit of things and people. They could have had a real juicy heart to heart discussion over the smell of that old chest.

"Bridget, its time for dinner." Bridget's mom called from the stairwell and then, with a sigh, went upstairs to her daughter's room. She knew Bridget was reading and couldn't possibly hear her. She leaned against the door with arms crossed and stared, smiling at her twelve-year-old daughter. She remembered being just like her when she was her age.

Bridget looked so cozy in the old overstuffed club chair, wide-eyed with fascination as she read. She tuned out everything and couldn't hear that her mother had called her to dinner three or four times.

Bridget was a voracious reader. She especially loved books about pioneers, the middle ages, anything Victorian; her hunger for the "olden days" was insatiable. If the words made her visualize the swirl of a long dress with five petticoats underneath and men who kissed the ladies' hands in greeting, she couldn't leave her soft chair even to eat!

She read so much that the summer after she turned eight she needed glasses. Bridget read a book a day; however, she wasn't a complete book-worm though. She also collected unusual miniatures, loved antique shopping (of course), sewing, training her pets, starting clubs with her friends and clothes shopping with her mom.

Bridget and her mom loved to go antique shopping whenever they had time and Bridget began to target hope chests. This came after reading many books about pioneers. She would run up to the front desk and anxiously ask the clerk if there were any old hope chests in their store. The old fashioned "fad" for acquiring a hope chest had an intriguing romantic appeal to Bridget; she was fascinated with the notion. But her mom made it clear that Bridget would have to save her own money. They were expensive.

Bridget was determined and very organized. She decorated a special jar and began saving earnestly. She saved her allowance, rented her comic books out to her brother, sold flower and vegetable seeds in the neighborhood and made extra money any way she could. But she was also impatient and needed to satisfy this strange craving in the meantime.

Bridget got the bright idea to turn the bottom drawer of her dresser into a hope drawer until she had a real chest. She painted that drawer to look like a hope chest with flowers bordering the sides and her name smack in the middle. It had to be obviously different from the rest of the dresser and it definitely was!

Then she began to collect things to put inside that she had read about. All, of course, for her future marriage to that gentleman who would kiss her hand at their first meeting. Their eyes would meet and they would fall in love at first sight. This 12-year-old was definitely a typical girl, dreaming and planning for the wedding that would make playing house real.

On her antique shopping excursions with her mom, Bridget would dream about things to put in that "hope drawer." Her Aunt Bessie gave her an antique silverware set. She decorated a cardboard box, polished that old silver till it gleamed, wrapped it in tissue and placed it in the drawer with high hopes. She found an ad in a magazine to buy a collection of recipe cards for $1 a month. It came with a special box and at the end of the year she would have it filled. It was perfect! She could be a great cook for that European gentleman. She sent for it and each month stowed those recipes in the special box in the drawer with high hopes. Actually, the hopes took up quite a bit of space in the drawer as well.

Bridget loved to sew with her mom who taught her how to master the old Singer sewing machine. She started a quilt, but realized there was no one in her neighborhood to have a quilting bee with, so she'd just have to plug away alone. She even put some of her old baby clothes in the drawer, hoping to put them on her own baby one day.

Chapter 2

One Sunday morning over breakfast Bridget's mom found an ad for an antique auction in the newspaper. Bridget was so excited that she got the newspaper wet in her oatmeal! The ad said there would be a variety of antique furniture items and she was wishing there would be a hope chest amongst all the old things. She had saved quite a bit of money and was anxious to see if she could buy one now.

The Sunday morning auction was full of people, but Bridget noticed there really weren't any kids, just a few toddlers being carried by their parents. Other kids didn't seem to be interested in antiques; but Bridget understood that, she knew she was different. She felt such an affinity with beautiful, old treasures. Her mom said it was because she taught Bridget that these things had character, soul and history, and carried the energy of elegance in their wooden lifetimes. Her mom also said that most parents probably didn't talk to their children this way.

This energy gave a home warmth and beauty that was not visible, but felt in ones bones. Bridget thought her mom sure was kooky in her philosophies and explanations but they always seemed to make total sense!

It was true, Bridget felt everything her mother had told her inside the auction where the energy was sky-high. The auction was held inside a huge, old barn, and the feeling of being surrounded by all these old things was delicious and exciting. A red farmhouse close to the barn made the scene look like something out of a picture book.

Once inside the huge, old barn, Bridget inhaled the great smell of hay and mustiness and smiled. She started walking through the rows of antiques and immediately spied it, an old hope chest that was breathtakingly beautiful!

The chest was a dark cherry wood with elegant, curved

feet that were meant to look like roots. Roses came up from the roots in each corner of the chest. The lid had a lip around it that curved up and down around the chest in the shape of an ivy vine. Detailed carvings of completely different gardens flanked the three sides. The front was carved to look like a garden gate and the lock was a real garden gate latch, except it was made of gold. It looked almost as if it were an old-fashioned holograph the way the latch popped out.

A skeleton key hung from the latch on a gold chain. The key was shaped like a rose and little thorns came out of it like the edges of a real key. The lid of the chest was a birds-eye view of a garden that was breath-taking. Looking at the chest made you want to meet the artist who sculpted such art out of wood. "Mom," she cried, "I found it, this is the one, over here. I have to have it, oh yes, yes, yes!"

Bridget jumped up and down with thumbs up, fists slamming into that 'yes' boxing punch that kids do to pound their excitement into the atmosphere. Her mom came running over grinning ear to ear, feeling the excitement her daughter was emanating.

"It is beautiful, Bridget." Her mom also stood in awe of the old hope chest. Bridget's cries brought the auctioneer running over.

"Young lady, if you don't settle down, I'll have to ask you to leave. This is an auction, not a cheerleading practice," he twirped with a shrill English accent.

But he saw that she was truly in awe of the antique and not just throwing a fit to get her parents out of there like so many other youngsters tried to pull. "I see you found something you like," he smiled. His attitude changed and softened. "It's an old Irish hope chest, came over on the boat with a load from Europe. It's extremely old and in fabulous condition for its age," he spoke as he tried to wave away gawking shoppers staring at the excited adolescent. Bridget's enthusiasm grew. "It's really from over there, from the books, I mean Europe, Ireland ?" she stammered. She couldn't believe it. Unfortunately she had caused such a commotion that people started admiring the chest and inspecting it inch by inch.

"Bridget, hush," Candace warned. "At an auction you don't want to show interest or you will have problems getting what you want." Her mom looked worried. She was going to let Bridget bid on the chest and she knew a loss would be horribly painful.

"Mom, does this mean, is it o.k.? Will you loan me the money if I don't have enough?" Bridget pleaded. "I'll do anything," she held her hands together in a desperate plea. The look on her face was equally as effective.

"Listen, Bridget, it is special but I'm not rich and I don't know how the bidding will go. It is very beautiful and in great shape for its age and a lot of people are obviously interested." Candace ushered her away, "let's try to find some other treasures, perhaps a hope chest more in our financial league."

"But Mom, I don't want to leave," Bridget couldn't take her eyes off the crowd around the chest as her mother pulled her away. "The bidding is going to start soon, let's finish looking around honey."

The English auctioneer started the auction and Bridget fidgeted nervously. After bidding was finished on a piano, a china hutch and a fainting couch, the hope chest was carried onto the stage.

"This old Irish hope chest has just arrived on American soil. It fared its journey well as you can see. It is almost two-hundred-years-old and very charming as many of you have noticed. It has captured the attention of numerous admirers." The auctioneer became melodramatic as he spoke the praises of the elegant piece. Bridget's mom whispered in her ear, "He knows the piece is popular and he's going to put it on a pedestal before he starts bidding."

Bridget's heart sank. She learned her lesson about keeping her mouth shut at an auction. Her mom noticed her long face and whispered again, " Bridget, even if you hadn't made a scene, it would still be very much in awe of everyone. It is just stunning and these people know a lovely piece when they see it."

The bidding began and very quickly Bridget knew she couldn't even nag her mother to bid. It would mean mortgaging their house. The bidding got more intense; it was a coveted piece. Soon it was between a very wealthy woman in a pink-feathered hat flashing lots of diamonds, and a gay antique dealer dressed in a smart Italian suit.

Suddenly, the bidding was interrupted by an old man in a very old-style European suit who quickly ascended the steps of the stage with the help of an elegant cane. He was short yet carried the elegance, sophistication and grace of a tall confident businessman. He was extremely old with lots of laugh lines and a few deep wrinkles, yet still handsome in a cute way. His gray hair, long for an elderly man, moved with each gesture of his face. He was almost comical even though he was distressed. He whispered frantically into the auctioneer's ear, but everyone could hear because the microphone was right there.

"I've changed me mind, I can't part with it. Do you

hear me? Stop the bidding, right now," his words had a deep Irish accent. Bridget began to giggle; she thought he sounded extraordinary. The crowd on the other hand was horrified, and a roar of complaints began to drown out the auctioneer's voice. The auctioneer placed his hand over the microphone and spoke frantically with the elderly man. Apparently he was trying to convince the Irishman to reconsider. The old man was adamant. The auctioneer returned to the microphone.

"I'm sorry, folks, I'm going to have to remove the chest from the auction," he beckoned the two weightlifters over who moved the piece off the stage and out the wide barn doors, with the old man following close behind them. It was quite baffling and the barn was abuzz with people whispering about the commotion.

"Please, people, silence, we will continue with our next piece, a beautiful Victorian armoire." He continued the auction with no explanation. Obviously the old Irish gentleman carried a lot of clout, for there were no questions, arguing or anything.

Bridget was very curious and quiet and she watched the old man and the hope chest leave the barn.

When the auction was over Bridget and her mom left the auction with some nice Irish antique linens. Her mom was talking about what they could make out of them while they walked back to their car. Bridget was quiet and sad. She couldn't think of anything but that hope chest. She knew she would never see anything like it again or ever love another one as much.

Suddenly, Bridget noticed the old Irish gentleman standing on an old tree stump looking frantically around the crowd. One hand was over his eyes shielding the glare of the sun and the other was on that cane trying to keep his balance on the stump.

"Mom, look, it's that old Irishman. He's going to fall he shouldn't be on that stump!" She ran towards him with Candace following. As she reached him she called, "Sir, don't. You'll fall. I'll help you!"

As soon as she spoke, he looked towards her and cried

out in that deep Irish accent. "There you are, I've wanted to find you, but I got worried as people started to disappear." He let Bridget help him off the stump and grinned from ear to ear.

"Bring your mother and come into the farmhouse kitchen for a cup of tea, I want to talk to you." Bridget just stared. Why in the world did this old man want to talk to her?

Bridget's mom came up and the old gentleman bowed his head and said, "How do you do, Ma'am. Me name's Timothy Klein and I'd like to invite you and your daughter in for tea. Have you an extra few minutes?"

Bridget's mom nodded her head but was as bewildered as her daughter. Timothy Klein put his arm through Bridget's skinny arm, leaned on his cane with the other arm and led them into the farmhouse kitchen. He asked the housekeeper to make some tea and motioned for the two of them to sit down at the old farmhouse table.

"I've come a long way at the prodding of my cousins who own this farm to sell an array of antiques from our family in Ireland. The only thing I had doubts about was the chest. It's very special. It's been in our family for two hundred years and I can't just let a total stranger buy it when I don't know who will be owning it, loving it and living with it."

He poured the tea that the housekeeper brought to the table and passed around slices of chocolate cake that he cut from the most beautiful crystal antique square cake plate on a pedestal. The glass sparkled with rainbows from the sunlight pouring in from the farmhouse kitchen windows. It was almost trancelike it was so elegant. Bridget and her mom found themselves politely gawking at the cake plate, the mouth-watering cake and the Irishman.

"In all of my 95 years I've watched the women of my family lovingly adore that chest and I'm the only one left. It has to be with someone who loves it like those women did." Bridget gobbled the delicious cake while staring wide-eyed at the deep green eyes of the man.

"When I noticed you fidget about the chest, I knew you

would love it like the women in my family." He smiled and Bridget and her mom giggled, remembering the scene she made was a tiny bit more than fidgeting.

"I want to give you the Klein family Irish hope chest because I know you will cherish it," he smiled that warm Irish smile again and his eyes glistened with tears. Bridget opened her mouth and chocolate cake fell out. Timothy Klein laughed a hearty laugh and her mother, speechless, tried to help mop up the mess with a napkin.

"Are you for real? Am I dreaming?"

"You aren't dreaming my dear, I'm quite certain that the life of the chest will continue in your possession."

Bridget stood up, knocking her chair down, ran to the old man and hugged him with all her might. Not letting go she said, "I fell in love with it the minute I saw it!" The auction bidding had made Bridget realize the value of the chest and she knew she was being given an extraordinary gift. She was silly with gratitude. She cried and shouted, "Yes, yes, yes," until the old man held his ears together. Bridget gave him every reason to believe he had made the right decision.

Bridget's mother was overwhelmed. "We'd like to pay you something for the chest," she stated.

Timothy Klein took her hands in his and firmly said, "No, the chest belongs with Bridget. It can't be sold. It must be given away and that's the way I want it. There will be no more fussing about it. There is an old Irish saying 'to give from the heart means to receive a thousand fold later'." He reached into his vest pocket and pulled out that key that Bridget had seen dangling from the chest. "Bridget, here is the key to lock up your treasures, I'll go get the weightlifters to put the chest in your mom's car."

The Hope Chest

Chapter 3

Soon Bridget had the exquisite hope chest in her room. It was so impressive that it looked like it belonged in a museum. She ran and got the furniture oil and a rag and began to polish the old wooden piece. Before long it took on a new glow; Bridget did a double take. Was it really glowing?! She rubbed her eyes and looked again.

"This can't be like Aladdin's lamp, can it?" she asked herself.

She quickly thrust open the lid of the trunk. No genie came out. Bridget shut the lid and gaped some more. The glow seemed to fade a little bit. She blinked long and hard. She shrugged her shoulders and went over to her hope drawer and pulled everything out. As Bridget opened the lid again, she began to place the quilt she was holding into the trunk.

The minute she let go of the quilt it was thrown out with such force it hit the ceiling sending her bedroom light a swinging. She gasped in disbelief. She must be imagining things! She closed her eyes, opened them and tried again. She picked up the box of silverware from Aunt Bessie and placed it inside but as soon as she let go, the silverware went flying out, spewing forks, spoons and knives everywhere.

Bridget covered her head with her arms and crouched down as the rain of flatware flew around the room. For a minute she sat there speechless, staring at the trunk. What was going on here? Was that old man a magician; was he playing tricks on her? She ran downstairs to her mom's phone book. She knew her Mom got his address so they could write him a thank you note. Her mom was at the market and Bridget wished she'd hurry home as she dialed the old Irishman.

"Mr. Klein, hello, this is Bridget, are you a magician? Are you playing tricks on me with the hope chest?" She was frantic and stumbled over her words.

"Calm down child, what's the matter?"

"Things are flying out of the chest. This is ridiculous. I don't know what to do. What is going on?"

"Child, you must be tired. You're imagining things. Lock the trunk up and take a nap, you have had an exciting and tiring day," he chuckled and hung up.

Bridget went back upstairs, stared at the trunk and picked up the mess. She wrapped everything up from the hope drawer into the quilt, threw the whole jumble in the trunk, slammed the lid down and quickly locked the chest. The chest rumbled and shook almost as if it were angry and the beautiful wood glowed like something indescribable.

Then an antique white embroidered ribbon came out of the key hole of the hope chest winding up into the air like a snake. A tiny, delicate hand emerged holding the ribbon and out came a beautiful girl about twelve inches high in a bubble. She hovered over the hope chest, not letting go of the ribbon, as though it were an umbilical cord. The bubble was like an Irish mist, fuzzy and cloudlike, which made Bridget keep rubbing her eyes as if she were imagining things.

"Who are you? A genie? A fairy godmother? What?" Bridget couldn't believe she was talking to her dream. She was dreaming, wasn't she?

"I'm not any of those things," the girl spoke with an Irish accent. She had long red hair wrapped in a ribbon just like the one she was holding onto. She had lovely fair skin that was almost translucent and piercing blue eyes; she was beautiful. She wore an old-fashioned white Irish linen dress much like the linens and fabric her mom had found at the auction.

"You're throwing your things into my chest." The girl angrily stood inside her bubble of fog with her hands on her hips.

"Your chest? Do you live in there?" Bridget sat down cross-legged, so she could be at eye-level with this small girl.

At that question the girl began to cry and tremble and

babble and Bridget couldn't understand her.

"Listen, sit down crisscross applesauce and talk to me. Maybe I can help," Bridget pleaded with the Irish redhead.

The girl calmed down a bit and said, "Do what?"

"Like me, sit down cross-legged and tell me what's the matter. It's the way my friends and I have serious discussions. What's your name? How did you get in there? What are you?" The red haired girl displayed characteristic temper. "What do you mean what am I? I'm a girl, just like you. Me name's Fairleigh," she snapped as she tried with great difficulty and finally successfully to sit down cross-legged like Bridget. "This isn't very lady-like. Your mother lets you sit this way?" She mopped up her tears with a pretty white handkerchief that looked exactly like one her mother purchased at the auction with all of those linens.

"I'm a regular girl, just like you, but I am older than you. I'm 17 and I was to be married on my 18th birthday. But I got very sick and thought I died but then realized when I saw you that I wasn't sure what had happened. All I know is that I seem to have been locked up in my hope chest, but all my things are gone! Only the hopes and dreams I have had for my life are inside here with me. Oh, I don't know. Do you suppose you could help me find my family?" She sadly wiped her eyes and then looked up at Bridget. "Why are you dressed in boys' clothes?"

Bridget looked down at her Levi's and flannel shirt. It was a cold day. She always dressed like that on cold days. She looked back up to the tiny Fairleigh in the fog bubble. "Fairleigh, what year is it?"

"Why 1799, of course, don't you know?" Fairleigh twisted at her handkerchief and looked at Bridget. Then she stood up and began to turn around carefully inspecting Bridget's bedroom.

"Fairleigh it is 2012, actually two hundred and 13 years later!"

Fairleigh turned around, looked at Bridget and began to

cry hysterically, "Me mother, me father, Connor." At the mention of the name Connor she cried even harder if that was possible.

"Who is Connor?" Bridget was almost in tears of sympathy listening to her cry.

"Me betrothed. We were to marry. I miss him so. They must all be dead."

"Listen, Fairleigh, I don't know what to do but I would like to help you. I have an idea. I got this hope chest from an old Irishman. He brought your chest over here to Missouri from Ireland. He says it has been in his family for two hundred years. Maybe he can help. His name is Timothy Klein."

"Twas me father's name, Timothy. But my last name is O'Hara."

"Get back in the chest, I'm going to go find him."

"I don't know how to get back in." She tugged at the ribbon that pulled her out.

"I bet this works backwards. Let's try to put you in the way you came out," said Bridget. With that she turned the key to unlock the trunk to help Fairleigh inside, and sure enough as she turned the key, the ribbon slowly pulled back inside the keyhole pulling Fairleigh with it. She disappeared.

Bridget just stared, awestruck at the whole thing and then pulled herself together. "I've got to help Fairleigh." She was determined. "Don't lose hope," she shouted at the chest, hoping Fairleigh could hear her.

Bridget ran to the kitchen and telephoned Timothy Klein. This time she was insistent. "Mr. Klein, you have to come over at once. I don't know what to do and I know you can help me," she spoke fast so he wouldn't hang up again.

"Child, I don't know what you're talking about," he said slowly as if he wanted Bridget to finish his sentence.

"It's about Fairleigh, she's stuck," Bridget almost shouted with desperation.

"I'll be right over," Mr. Klein said. It was as though she had muttered a magic word.

"O.k. here's my address."

The doorbell rang shortly thereafter. Bridget just stared at Mr. Klein and then repeated, "Are you a magician, are you playing tricks with me with that hope chest?"

"I believe it's polite to say hello and invite me in," said Mr. Klein, "and no, I am not a magician and no, you are not dreaming. I had to wait until I knew that you knew to help you. But really, I can't help you, you have to help us, I mean her." He sat down on the living room sofa holding that elegant cane in both hands between his knees. Bridget noticed the cane had two emeralds for eyes and the head looked like an artist's sculpture of an old man--actually it looked a lot like Mr. Klein.

"Are those real emeralds? And are you real?" Bridget pulled the ottoman close to Mr. Klein and sat cross-legged on it staring at him wide-eyed.

Timothy Klein's eyes twinkled, " I'm so glad you found Fairleigh. After your first phone call I had to make sure you were sure and that you had found her. Listen to me carefully. When I found the trunk in our attic of our family home I also found

Fairleigh, but she appeared as a doll and didn't move or speak. I found her likeness in an old family photo album, that is how I knew her name."

Bridget told him the whole story and invited him upstairs. She turned the key in the lock and out came the foggy bubble with Fairleigh in it. Timothy Klein didn't take his eyes off the small girl.

"I can't believe it. How did you make her talk?" He reached out to touch Fairleigh but his hand just went right through her like a ghost.

"I don't know, I just polished and rubbed the chest and when I turned the key out she came," Bridget sat down again so she could look Fairleigh in the eye. She tugged at Timothy Klein's coattails to make him sit down with her. Fairleigh had already accomplished the crisscross applesauce stance and stared at Timothy waiting for him to sit down.

"We can't talk seriously until you sit this way," Fairleigh said matter of factly in her cute Irish accent. They all laughed and then Fairleigh said, "I need help. Who are you and are you from Ireland?"

"Me name is Timothy Klein and I am your great, great grandnephew. You my dear, are my great, great Aunt Fairleigh."

Fairleigh stared wide-eyed at him. She began to cry again sobbing, "I'm dead, I'm dead."

"Now listen," Timothy said very kindly, "we want to help you but we haven't a clue. All I can tell you is a little voice inside me heart told me to stop the auction and give the chest to this here little American girl Bridget. I'll answer any questions I can but I don't know what to do meself. You did die and you were buried in the family cemetery in Ireland. So it isn't as if you disappeared."

"It is as if her soul is here. Like maybe there was some unfinished business that you had to deal with," Bridget pondered, twisting her hair as she spoke. "Now, I'm no psychologist obviously but I love to read my daddy's 'Psychology Today' magazine a lot. Tell us all about yourself and anything that made you especially sad or frustrated; then we'll brainstorm and figure out what to do." Bridget ran to get her school notebook and a pencil and sat back down again, pencil poised.

"Well, what have I got to lose? I guess I'm a ghost," Fairleigh looked off into space with a very sad face and tears streamed down her beautiful pale face. She slowly turned toward Bridget and began to tell her story. "I had so many high hopes me whole life." With elbow on her knee, Fairleigh put her chin on her hand and looked faraway in the distance as she spoke.

"I wanted more than ever to marry me friend from when we were little lambs, Connor. We'd known each other all our lives and I loved him with all my heart, but he had an even bigger heart than me." She began to cry again; her hanky was soaked.

"Then there was me best friend Lucy, her family was Protestant and hated my family. I wanted her to be me maid of honor. I loved her like a sister. We could talk about anything. She was wonderful. I loved her so. But it got to the point where our families forbade us to see one another. Glory be, 'twasn't as if WE were to marry. We were just friends. 'Twas ridiculous. Let's see, unfinished business, I guess that is why a soul would return, to finish their business. But what about Connor? I know he is my soul mate." She wept some more.

"This is good, keep talking. Anything you can think of. Can you remember anything else?" Bridget wrote furiously.

"It's hard to think of things, I spent so much time trying to be the judge for me brother and sister. All they did was fight. It was stupid and selfish. It made me crazy. I loved them both and got along with them alone, but the two of them together were like two roosters, fighting without any reason.

"Then there were me parents, what a tizzy mess, they also fought like two mad dogs, me life was quite a hailstorm. That's why I loved Connor so much, things were always so calm with him. He had high hopes and dreams of making life better for us, my family and friends, everyone. What a lovely soul he was. His soul touched mine and I don't know how to describe that feeling but it is the most lovely feeling. It's softer than a baby bunny and it goes through your body to your soul and I don't know how to describe it other than that.

"I just know when we spoke, he didn't have to touch me with his hand, but his soul touched mine and it was better than holding hands or kissing. Although I loved that," Fairleigh glanced at us as though she just remembered we were there, blushing bright red and then started to cry again.

Bridget passed a tissue box not even thinking a second thought about it, and funny thing, Fairleigh grabbed one through the foggy bubble and was actually able to use it! It was very strange because when Timothy tried to touch her, his hand went through the bubble and Fairleigh. She was a hologram, or was she?

"I can't believe it, hankies in a box," she marveled at the tissue and then mopped up her tears. Suddenly Bridget could feel her goodness inside of her soul. She was sweet and true and real and honest. She just felt it. It was nice. Fairleigh looked deep into Bridget's eyes and they knew they could trust each other.

Bridget knew she couldn't ask just any psychologist for help. It had to be someone who believed in aliens, outerspace, and spiritual stuff.

"Fairleigh, I have to think about how to help you. Stay in the hope chest and I'll be back later. Mr. Klein, have you any idea what to do?" Bridget asked.

"No, I don't, but I'll think about it. She is two hundred years older and she did die, perhaps she is just a ghost. I'm very confused, maybe we should call in a good Irish priest," Mr. Klein drummed his fingers on his chin and looked puzzled. Little did he know that a priest was just what Bridget had in mind.

"I'll call you Mr. Klein, but right now it's time for me to be Harriet the Spy." She walked him to the front door and returned to Fairleigh.

"I don't think he has a clue," Fairleigh was wringing her tissue now and pacing in the air above the hope chest.

"Fairleigh, he did have a good idea. I'm off to find the neighborhood priest and whoever else can help. I'll be back."

Bridget turned the key and Fairleigh waved as she got pulled back into the keyhole.

Chapter 4

Bridget ran downstairs to the garage, threw her notebook into the basket of her bike and took off as fast as she could, ponytail flying behind her in the warm spring wind. It was a beautiful day. Bridget rode to the Catholic church at the end of her block. It was a beautiful, huge old brick church covered with patches of ivy and two giant magnolia trees in the front with those giant white flowers. Below the trees, the front lawns were covered with a soft grass in which the neighborhood children loved to lay down. In the hot summer months, the grass under the cool shade of the trees was delicious.

Luckily the priest was Irish. Bridget knew him fairly well. She ran inside the ominous building looking for him. The church was cool and dark and she could smell the candles burning. Church music was playing softly in the background. It was sort of like a haunted house but it felt safe, not scary. She couldn't find the priest and decided to peek inside one of the confessionals. Luckily it was empty and Bridget whispered into the curtained divider.

"Father Bailey, are you here?"

"In confession it isn't necessary to use names, just state your sins and we'll speak about the corrections," a deep familiar Irish voice explained.

It was him. "Father, it's me Bridget O'Riley, I have to talk to you, it's important."

Two eyes peeked through the veiled cloth. "Aye, it's you, Bridget. I'll meet you outside."

Soon, two blue eyes twinkled with the friendly smile of the older but still very handsome Father Bailey. He was very tall and as he crouched down to look Bridget in the eye, the soft folds of his black priestly robe brushed up against Bridget's arm. Though it lasted just a moment, the intuitive 12-year-old felt the kindness of the priest's soul brush up against her arm with the cloth. She hoped he could help.

"Father, I have a strange problem and lots of questions about Ireland long ago." Bridget fidgeted. She didn't rehearse what to say and didn't even know how to say it.

"Come Bridget, sit down and tell me all about it," Father Bailey sat down in a pew in the middle of the church; the tall ceilings made the whole ordeal formidable. The echoing of their voices also made Bridget's words sound more intense and real.

Bridget sat down, took a deep breath and began. The words just spilled out, "Father, is there such thing as a ghost, and can they be very tiny, and do they exist in Ireland and can they be two-hundred-years-old, and can we help them go where they belong, and are they lost souls?"

The priest laughed heartily, he had the most wonderful laugh, warm and inviting just like his personality. "Bridget, hold on, one question at a time. Ghosts don't normally appear to people and actually speak, but after someone dies a family member often feels their presence. We don't know what size they are. No one has ever told me they've actually seen one, just felt the spirit like a person hovering over your shoulder watching you write. A ghost and a spirit are essentially the same thing. It is just that movies make them scary and white like a sheet over a child on Halloween. It is our silly human thinking of what a ghost looks like. I believe if you could see a ghost or spirit that it would look like the person when they were alive except perhaps translucent, like you could put your hand through them."

Father Bailey looked around the church quickly and then whispered very quietly to Bridget, "Don't say anything, if the Bishop were to hear me say that he would scold me!"

Bridget smiled, glad that he was so human and so real, "But Father, why would a ghost appear?"

"Perhaps Bridget, because they had some unfinished business and they were reluctant to leave. They were not ready. That is why we pray for the dead. The prayers help them loosen the ties and go where they belong."

"But Father, what about magic, do you believe in magic?"

"No, Bridget, magic is a trick. In Ireland our magicians were lots of fun. Many of them attributed their magic to leprechauns. But that's a myth. It is a folktale. No one has ever seen a leprechaun. It's Irish silliness. Listen, my dear, if you believe you are feeling the presence of a spirit, you must first pray for your own protection, that you don't become entangled in their mess. Then pray daily and light candles for the soul. You will help the spirit in this way." Father Bailey rose, blessed Bridget with the sign of the cross, hugged her and went back to the confessional booth.

"Thank you, Father," she called after him. She adored that priest, but she knew he couldn't help her with Fairleigh. But she did resolve to pray more frequently during this adventure she was caught up in. Bridget ran outside, got her bike and pedaled quickly to her friend Esther's house. Desperate measures called for special help and Esther was the best.

The Hope Chest

Chapter 5

Bridget smiled, thinking about her relationship with Esther and the story that Fairleigh had told her about her best friend Lucy back in Ireland. It was the same story with parents and religion several hundred years later. This prejudice had to stop. Bridget hoped she and her friends were a beginning to the end of hatred and separation. Bridget loved her friends for who they were and how they treated her, not what color skin they had or what religion they practiced. Bridget hid her bike behind a shrub and ran around to the side of the house and began throwing pebbles at her friend's window.

Esther's family was Jewish and very religious and didn't like the fact that the two girls were so close. If Bridget rang the bell her mother would probably say Esther was busy and couldn't play. The two girls even had a code if they had to phone each other. They would dial, let the phone ring once, hang up and dial back. Otherwise Esther's parents wouldn't let them speak. They were afraid that if Esther had non-Jewish friends she would rebel against the strict rules of their observant household. They said they couldn't risk a non-Jewish friendship in their home. The girls still adored one another and thought the parents' attitude was ridiculous.

Bridget whispered loudly, "Esther, are you there?"

The pebbles gently got her friend's attention. Curly-headed Esther pushed her face up against the screen, "Meet me in my brother's treehouse," she mouthed back.

Bridget ran to the gate at the side of the house, pushed open the latch and ran out back. She ran through the expansive grassy backyard to the large oak that grew at the back of the lush garden. She climbed the twisting steps of the treehouse.

Esther's brother was studying to be an architect and he had built the most amazing tree house for an architectural school project. The focus of the project was to oppose a cultural tradition. Esther's brother Ben had quite a sense of humor and he created a "Parent Proof" dwelling allowing kids to have control. He decided to oppose childproofing. His focus was a giant old oak in the back yard and it was there that he built "Bahyeet Yeladeem," Hebrew for "The Children's House."

Their parents could never get up the winding steps of the treehouse. Ben was so smart he could be called a geek if you were talking to him on the phone, but once you saw him in person your opinion changed drastically. Esther's friends called him a hunk and he was. He spent an hour every day at the gym much to the wrath of his parents' anger who thought that time could be used in Torah (biblical) study. But he made time for both. He was tall, muscular and very handsome. He had the same curly hair as Esther, twinkling eyes that danced with humor and mishchief, one big dimple on his right cheek, full lips and a wonderful command of the neighborhood kids.

He was king as far as they were concerned! He also

dressed modestly, always in a white button-down oxford shirt, (but short-sleeved so he could work), and tan khakis with the traditional 'tzi,tzim' strings hanging out. Orthodox Jewish men always wear these holy strings and hold them as they say their prayers. They swung in the wind as he worked outside. Often, they were dirty with sawdust, twigs and leaves clinging on to the religious strings as he worked on that treehouse.

The treehouse had lots of humorous twists, that if a parent did manage to climb into it, they would never want to get up into it again (IF they could get down!) The secrets of the treehouse required a neighborhood kid meeting with Esther's brother Ben where he swore all the kids to secrecy. They were easy enough to keep secret because no kid wanted their parents up there! They also greatly respected this "big college kid" who was still somewhat of a teenager yet on the border of becoming an adult.

There was a hidden lever disguised as a book, on a bookshelf, right inside the treehouse entrance at the top of the stairs. If you pushed the book onto its right side it tripped all the stairs down and the entire twisty staircase turned into a slide. This made for quick exits as well as a great parent deterrent.

If a parent did manage to get in, Ben instructed the one who was closest to the bookshelf to quickly and quietly stand with their backs hiding the secret book and to reach behind and push the book down. The parents had to slide down since none of the kids seemed to know how those stairs were tripped! They all blamed it on Ben's architectural madness! This did not appeal to parents at all. They quickly resorted to shouting from the grass if they wanted one of their kids.

If the book lever was pushed left in the OTHER direction, the first ten feet of the stairs from the ground would collapse and be pulled up a rope that ran through the middle of them, like dominoes on a chain. If you were being followed you only had to push the book lever and voila! Not many people could jump ten feet to reach the rest of the twisty staircase.

Once a parent was inside they weren't very comfortable

anyway. The ceilings were too low and they had to crouch inside. That was, at least, only until the adults were out. Another lever made this false low ceiling collapse into the wall. When it was down the high ceilings made the treehouse open and airy. Of course parts of the ceiling came down as well. This was wonderful for counting the stars during summer sleepovers in the treehouse.

The treehouse was safe and the girls often played there secretly. It was huge and roomy and built well. Bridget loved it as did any child who was lucky enough to play in it. There were a couple of trapdoors, a secret loft and one open loft. Ben said this secret loft was built in honor of the Jews that were hidden in attics during the Holocaust. These two lofts were amazing. None of the neighborhood kids knew about the secret loft except Esther's family and Ben's professors. Of course Esther told Bridget because they were best friends. Bridget knew she would take the secret to her grave in honor of the reasons for which it was built; and above all else she was a trustworthy and true blue friend to Esther.

Needless to say Ben was one of the top architectural students in his class and won a huge honor for the project.

Esther came running out of the house with her soft brown curls bouncing and scurried up the winding steps. She wore a plain, light blue jumper that fell well below her knees and a white, long-sleeved blouse underneath. The top button of the blouse was fastened to hide her neck. This style of dress is called 'frumme'. Orthodox Jews dressed modestly, and girls and women had to cover their knees and elbows. She wasn't allowed to wear pants or short sleeves, and all her dresses were long. She had huge, deep brown, mystical eyes and long, curly hair that went past her shoulders. A few short curls hung as bangs. She was always pulling on a strand of hair next to her ear until it was held straight, then let it go and it would bounce back into a curl.

She kissed her friend on both cheeks as was the custom of her family. Bridget loved that about Esther, she was so European, like all those books. Bridget took hold of her friend's hands and they sat down together criss crossed. Esther knew right away something huge was up and Bridget knew that Esther knew. They shared the feeling that they were soul mate friends. They were very close and often knew what the other was thinking.

Bridget smiled, loving the fact that her friend knew something was up, "Esther, you are going to find this hard to believe but you have to because I need your help."

"Bridge, you know I will believe you. Spill it."

Bridget took a deep breath and told Esther the whole story. Esther's eyes widened with wonder. She was incredibly intuitive and Bridget couldn't wait to hear what her friend had to say.

"Bridge, take me to her. I have to meet her," and with that last word, Esther was already climbing down the steps. Bridget ran after her. The girls jumped on their bicycles and the two pedaled quickly towards Bridget's house.

Chapter 6

Halfway down the block Esther screeched her bike to a halt. "Bridge we have to get Natalie first, I have a feeling we'll need her." Natalie was their Philipina friend who they considered to be their third spiritual soulmate. The trio met in a strange way at the park during summer vacation.

Esther and Bridget were practicing what they called their "seventh sense" game where they sat cross-legged facing each other with their hands pressed up against each other's. They pressed their hands together finger to finger, closed their eyes and focused on telepathy.

Suddenly they were interrupted by a little finger tapping on each of their shoulders. At first they ignored it because little kids often came up and poked them and wondered what they were doing. But this finger persisted.

They opened their eyes to a little Philipino girl about their age with straight long black hair, almond shaped black eyes and a cute mischievous smile. She wore capri jeans, white tennis shoes and a pink t-shirt that said "Angel." Her skin was a golden brown and she tossed her head to get her long black hair out of the way. She was elegant in the way she moved her hair and body and was obviously "a girls' girl," feminine and proud of it. She was squatting on the ground and looked back and forth to Esther and Bridget.

"Can I show you a couple of tricks?" her soft little voice sparkled with eagerness.

Bridget and Esther glanced at each other, smiled and knew at once they had found a comrade, a mate, a partner in crime so to speak. Without words the girls moved positions and Natalie gently sat down cross legged between the girls, forming a triangle. Natalie put one of her hands against Esther and one against Bridget, so each girl had one hand pressed up against the others'. They still hadn't even introduced themselves.

Natalie softly spoke, "now to start; focus on your index finger--this leads to your heart and the focus on this will tell you someone's intentions – good or evil." The girls all pressed harder against each other's index finger.

Natalie smiled, tossed her head and laughed, "I didn't need to do this with you two, I felt it when I saw you both. I just wanted to teach you. After you get good at this, your intuition gets stronger and you won't even need to do this. Now press the middle fingers together, this leads to action. If we decide on a plan, this helps decide if we go for it or we stop and figure something else out.

"When a bunch of us does this together, it works better and the messages are stronger and faster. I can't do that alone, can you girls? Of course, I always ask for a white light to protect us and give us the answer that God would want," she giggled, "that part my mom insists on." Bridget gasped, "My Mom tells me that too!" The girls smiled.

"Now the fourth fingers, or ring finger, carries messages but it takes a lot of practice. Let's try." Natalie squeezed her eyes so tightly they almost disappeared into her face.

"N!" Esther and Bridget squealed simultaneously.

"That's right!" Natalie beamed. "Keep going!" She squeezed her eyes again.

"A!" they squealed again.

"Good," Natalie pressed on to spell her name but was interrupted by a loud piercing, "Natalie, where are you?" Obviously Natalie's mom was looking for her.

"Darn, she gave it away," Natalie snapped her fingers and stood up, "you girls are good!" she smiled and ran off to her mother.

After that the girls saw Natalie in the park frequently and the three became fast friends. They adored her and she, them. Esther's parents were not too keen on the idea of another friend outside of their religion but Natalie convinced them that world peace could never be accomplished if people would not make friends outside of their groups. They were astonished at the wisdom coming out of this young pre-teen child but who could argue with that? When Esther and Bridget asked her how she learned this stuff she just shrugged her shoulders and said, "it's just in my head."

Bridget and Esther turned around and wheeled the few blocks toward Natalie's house.

They heard her practicing her flute in the living room and pounded on the front door. Natalie came running to the door.

"What's up you two?"

Esther and Bridget each grabbed an arm and pulled their friend out onto the front porch. "You have to come with us, we'll explain on the way, get your bike," Bridget grabbed the flute and tossed it onto a chair in the foyer. Esther ran to the open garage and grabbed Natalie's bike helmet and lunged for her bike. She was quite a sight in that long skirt she wore. Bridget laughed, "Esther, you need a pair of jeans!" Esther shot a look at Bridget and said, "Yeah, right!"

The three girls pedaled madly down the street. What a sight they were, so different, yet such great friends; they smiled at each other as they rode. They loved the differences in one another and respected each others' home lives for their differences. They giggled and squealed and almost crashed into each other several times in the course of telling the story to Natalie.

Once they arrived at Bridget's they didn't even take time to properly kickstand their bikes up, they threw them on the front lawn and rushed up the stairs. They dashed into the room where Esther and Natalie stood staring at the hope chest.

"Oh my, Bridget, it's more than you've ever wanted. It's grand," said Esther. She walked all around it then suddenly cried, "pull the club chair in front of the door, don't let anyone in." She and Natalie helped Bridget push the chair against the door.

Bridget could never tell if Esther was being dramatic or she had an 'instinct rush' as the girls liked to call it. Esther had sudden flashes of what was going to happen and she would call out 'instinct rush.' The girls would giggle and huddle in a whisper or run somewhere private to discuss it. Esther was also dramatic which was attributed to the fact she was a Gemini and full of enthusiasm and had a flare for excitement. Natalie had her arms spread as wide as she could with her hands on the hope chest, fingers spread out and eyes closed.

"Hush you two, I'm trying to get a feel for this chest," Natalie whispered.

"Sit down girls, you have to meet Fairleigh." Esther pulled Natalie off the chest and the two girls sat down criss crossed while Bridget turned the key in the old lock. Out came the ribbon with little Fairleigh latched on tight. Bridget introduced the two. "Fairleigh, these are my best friends Esther and Natalie. They're going to help us."

Fairleigh stared a little warily at Esther and Natalie and with her eyes fixed on Esther, she spoke to Bridget, "Can I trust this girl and why does she look this way?"

Bridget began to explain to Fairleigh that Esther was an Orthodox Jew, then suddenly stopped speaking and gasped. Esther had stuck her hand out to shake Fairleigh's hand and had actually grasped it. Fairleigh was just as shocked. She herself thought she was an apparition. Then it was Esther's turn to gasp. She turned to Bridget without letting go of Fairleigh, "Oh Bridget, I feel her energy. She's alive. She's not a ghost. She's good, we can trust her." Natalie tried and was also able to grasp her hand, then Bridget followed and then Fairleigh giggled at their amazement.

Esther looked back at Fairleigh, all smiles and glowing. Fairleigh was puzzled and looked at Bridget, "Please translate. I can't understand her Orthodox language!" The three 12-year-old girls laughed and whispered a little bit, shook hands and then Bridget explained.

"Fairleigh, we don't tell many people this because when we used to tell some friends when we were younger they just made fun of us. We've decided to tell you though. We call each other our soul mate friends not just because we're best friends but because we feel and sense things other people don't.

Esther, Natalie and I feel vibrations of a person from shaking their hands, feeling their clothes, touching something that belongs to them and sometimes being in their house or bedroom. We know whether they are good or bad, kind or mean, and sometimes other things, too. It doesn't matter that I'm Irish Catholic like you or Jewish like Esther or Philipino like Natalie. Special people are born into all kinds of families. We're just lucky we found each other." The three clenched each other's hands, smiled at one another and looked back to Fairleigh and spoke simultaneously: "We want to help you together." They looked at each other, laughed and yelled "Jinx!"

Fairleigh's mouth was agape, she half fell down in a heap in her bubble. Suddenly the three girls heard the voices of Bridget's mother and Timothy Klein coming up the stairs. The three of them covered their mouths with their hands when they heard what the Irishman had to say.

"When your daughter called me this afternoon about the worms in the wood of the old chest I was so sad. I had to call customs and notify them and they said I had to bring the chest down right away to be fumigated. If it isn't done according to their procedure and we can't kill all the worms and the larvae, they'll have to burn the chest. I'm so sorry Mrs. O'Riley, I could just cry knowing how much your daughter loves the old chest. Me, myself, I love the old chest, I will cry if anything happens like that, but what can I do? Me hands are tied!"

Suddenly the girls understood. Timothy Klein had realized that Bridget had discovered the secret of the old chest and was obviously trying to get it back and destroy it. He was manipulating Bridget's mother. Natalie whispered, "but then why did he take the risk of giving you the hope chest in the first place?" The girls shrugged their shoulders and Bridget put her fingers to her mouth, "shhhhhhhh."

"Bridget will have to understand. Here's her room. The chest is in here. I certainly don't want some Irish termite to invade our home." The doorknob turned but the club chair kept the door from opening.

"Bridget, are you in here? Open this door at once, it's very important. I have Mr. Klein here and we need to speak to you!"

The three girls looked at each other in shock. "It's a trick," whispered Fairleigh frantically, "quick, get inside the chest."

Bridget and Esther hopped into the hope chest. Natalie had one foot poised in the air about to climb in when she realized she wouldn't fit, there just wasn't room for three.

"Come on," both girls pulled her trying to squeeze her in, but it was no use. Three girls could not fit in that hope chest.

"Listen you two," Natalie squealed as they tried pulling her, "I need to stay outside to distract your mom and that old Irishman," she pulled away from their grasp and landed kerplunk on the floor. The looks the three exchanged in sadness and friendship were heartbreaking. Natalie stood up and lovingly put her hands on each girl's cheek and then whispered, "Be quiet" and shut the lid. Bridget's hunch was right.

"Oh, I was hoping and I was right," she held onto Esther's arm with one hand, Esther hung onto Bridget's arm and with the other hand she locked the chest from the inside.

"Esther I was right, it does lock this way." The latch clicked shut and the chest rumbled, shook and glowed. A bubble mist filled the inside of the chest. It was thick like glue and then they heard Fairleigh's voice.

"Bridget, Esther, rub the mist all over you, and wish you were invisible. Put some in your pockets, we may need it later. It will protect you," Fairleigh could only be heard. They couldn't see her. Esther and Bridget rubbed the stuff, which felt very soft all over themselves.

"Fairleigh," Bridget whispered, "how do you know about this soft glue?"

" 'Twas by accident really," Fairleigh's voice was penetrating the entire chest, like a stereo; she could be heard from every fiber of the wood.

"When I first heard Timothy Klein's voice I was so scared I was flitting about in this mist and waving my arms about wishing aloud I was part of the wood and I came out a doll. Later on I wished I could float through the keyhole and I quickly realized this glue was a wishing glue and quite helpful.

From outside the hope chest Natalie was astonished to watch the chest rumble and vanish. She sunk into the club chair hoping her weight would help to keep out Mr. Klein and Bridget's mom. She didn't know what else to do – she needed to think.

The Hope Chest

Chapter 7

From inside the chest the girls heard Timothy Klein and Mrs. O'Riley's voices drifting further and further away and after what seemed like an hour, the hope chest lid thrust open. Bridget and Esther, still huddled together with eyes closed tightly, ventured a peek out. They stood up and stepped out of the chest and found themselves in a beautiful green meadow outside. It seemed very real, yet different somehow.

"Esther we're in Ireland, I know it," Bridget took her friend's hand and they stepped out in to the meadow. It was a beautiful grassy green meadow. Suddenly they heard Fairleigh and looked back toward the hope chest. Out she came through the key hole still in her bubble but this time she was life size!

"We're home," Fairleigh twirled about, beautiful and

proud of her new figure.

"How did we get here Fairleigh, what happened?" Bridget and Esther were astonished by the life size Fairleigh.

"Bridget, I think it 'twas me hopes," Fairleigh said, "I found something out quite by mistake and a bit of luck. I was pondering me situation during all that rumbling when I noticed a funny itch on me back. It's been bothering me for some time. It 'twas this button. Do ye know what this is?"

She held the button up high for them to see. It looked like an ordinary linen covered button but the underside and edges were beveled glass. It was beautiful, almost like a diamond. "It tisn't an ordinary button. It's a leprechaunic button. This is how those nasty little green men held me under their spell. I ripped it off and me memory has been tumbling back. You know, you folk think those leprechauns are only out for their gold, but their magic is quite different from ordinary magic. They have a grasp of things most humans either don't believe or ignore."

"But fact of the matter is they know more than any of

us. In Ireland, in my day, we believed it. We certainly didn't ignore it, but we didn't know the secrets. We knew the secrets took faith in what you couldn't see but we had no access to their knowledge. This is why everyone always wanted to catch a leprechaun. Not just for the gold but for the secrets.

"They have a religion called Kabala and the book filled with all the secrets is called the Zohar. We have some myths about people that have succeeded in catching one here and there but I'll tell you about that later. Right now we haven't much time and we have lots of work to do and I need your help." Fairleigh stopped suddenly then said, "Stop, listen."

Off in the distance beyond a group of trees they heard the music. It was lilting and magical and many men were singing.

"It's the leprechauns, they're planning something. It's the dance of the leprechauns. Hurry, we must hide. They mustn't find us or we're doomed. Help me hide the hope chest."

The girls heaved and shoved and moved the chest behind a clump of bushes. They peered out of the bushes toward the music. They could hear it loud and clear now.

"Listen to me girls," Fairleigh whispered, "I used to think it was a myth, the whole lot of me village did too, but obviously it isn't. Legend has it that they abused the secrets – they were meant for good use. It also says some evil leps brainwashed their prince after the king died and the whole world of leps turned into an evil army. The story is that the leprechauns were really a mean bunch, not do-gooders that granted wishes. They hated to give wishes and gold because it drained their magical abilities. They lost the desire to receive in order to share. They only wanted to receive and hoard and when they lost their generosity they began to lose the gifts. Myth has it, if they continued to share and not hoard, they would not lose their gifts, but receive more than their share. Do you understand?

"Listen to their song, it gives it all away. They'll do anything to keep their magic to themselves. They cast some kind of curse over me; I never died and I was never sick. They made me sick and put me in my chest. They wanted to get rid of me because I found them out and began to learn their secrets. I realized that anyone could learn these secrets and be happier but they didn't want this to happen.

"That's why I was cursed and put under the spell inside my hope chest. My hopes and dreams were what kept me alive in there Bridget. I'm alive again now that you made my hopes and dreams come true. You saved me, Bridget! That Timothy Klein only hoped to take me far from my home. What he thought would keep me away backfired on him. Now my only hopes are that it is 1799 in Ireland and I can find my family. Let's listen; follow me."

The girls followed Fairleigh, still in her bubble but now life size, behind a closer clump of bushes to listen to the song and watch the dance of the leprechauns.

They danced around a huge bonfire that blazed bright green, not the usual yellowish-orange flames that Bridget and Esther were used to. The leprechauns stomped around the fire, about thirty of them, obviously very angry. Bridget wondered what could have possibly made them so angry?

"We're mad, we're mad, we're the leprechauns and we're mad.

We hate the Irishmen, they want nothing but our pot of gold and wishes.

They become glad and we are so sad.

Who do they think they are, demanding OUR gold and our wishes, tsk tsk?

Never again, no more, no more, they're nothing but thieves.

They know no respect, they could careless. Who do they think they are?

We're little green men, with lives of our own, we're not four-leaf cloverleaves.

Nor are we wishes on candles or wishes on stars.

We're mad, we're mad, now the pretty one has stolen our prince,

She has taken his heart

And he's left our province.

We must force them apart!"

At that last sentence they all stopped, turned toward the bonfire and threw in what looked like green letters into the bonfire. There was an explosion into a rainbow of fireworks which landed like different colors of rain and the leprechauns ran around in circles with hands, faces and tongues outstretched sucking up the colored rain. The angry looks left their faces and the leader climbed up on a tree stump while the rest sat down in front of him to listen.

"Now that you have all calmed down," the leader motioned them with his hands to sit and gather around, "it is time to make a plan. You have all ingested the secret letters of inspiration and now it is time to let them come forth as ideas for our plan to get our prince back. I know our creativity knows no bounds now. Please take a moment to meditate and allow the letters to combine into words and ideas. After a few minutes I will take turns with all of you as you speak."

The leprechauns sat like little yogis and sang Li Li Li Li Li Li Li Li over and over as they swayed back and forth with eyes closed. The leader's little daughter walked about with a maid servant passing out clear glass mugs of a frothy, steaming, bubbling green drink which she placed beside each leprechaun. As they meditated, they paused every minute or so and sipped the strange looking liquid.

Bridget, Esther and Fairleigh were stone cold staring without blinking at the scene. They were mesmerized. Suddenly Fairleigh shook herself from the trance and waved her hands in front of Bridget and Esther's faces.

"Snap out of it, do you hear me? It's magic and we'll get hypnotized." She jumped up and frantically grabbed a hand of each girl and ran toward the village.

Bridget gasped, "Where are we going?" The two girls were breathless as they ran with Fairleigh.

"To my house if it's still there."

They ran through the beautiful soft grassy meadows,

through heather, up and down a hill and then another hill. At the top the three stopped, out of breath and staring down at a tiny village full of sheep and grass-thatched roofs.

Down a cobblestone path they ran and Fairleigh led them into a beautiful old round red barn. It was unusual and quaint, something out of a picture book. Fairleigh pushed the girls up a ladder into a hay filled loft where they tumbled breathless and fell backwards, arms and legs outstretched, exhausted.

Fairleigh held up the button. "You two have to help me figure out how to break this spell."

"Not until you get us something to drink," Bridget gasped, Esther nodded in agreement.

Fairleigh looked at the two of them, giggled and said, "I'm sorry I've lost me manners, I'll tell you where the well is."

"That's o.k., just tell us where a water fountain is," Esther said matter of factly, trying to unrumple herself. Fairleigh took her by the shoulders, "Esther, that is our water fountain. You'll have to bring a bucket with you and bring some back for us."

"Is the bucket kosher?" she asked as a matter of habit when she wasn't home.

Fairleigh looked at her confused. Suddenly they heard a voice and Fairleigh shushed them.

A young man walked into the barn and was talking to himself while kicking straw around. He covered his face with his hands, collapsed onto the barn floor and began crying. He was tall and from what they could make out from their position, he appeared handsome. He was dressed in grey, wool knickers with suspenders and a white, long-sleeved Irish linen shirt. The fabrics were rich and the suspenders were studded with what looked like green emeralds. On his shiny black boots were pewter buckles embedded with larger green emeralds.

Fairleigh's hands flew to her cheeks. She cried out, "Connor," and practically flew off of the loft. The young man stopped crying and looked up, jumped up and caught her in his arms. He twirled her around, covered her face with kisses and the fog bubble disappeared! They both talked at once, hugging and crying until they both shut up and kissed each other over and over again. Bridget and Esther had to cover their eyes, but of course, peeked out between their fingers!

They finally stopped kissing and held each other's faces in their hands then both began speaking at once again. They laughed and finally Fairleigh spoke, "Connor, I thought I was dead. I was under a cursed spell, the leprechauns, they put me in my hope chest and I had no idea what had happened to me until I eventually found this button. When I tore it off my memory came back and I knew I had been trapped and cursed. Some friends helped me and I just got back. How long have I been gone? Do you know what happened to me? Help me, Connor!"

Connor let go of Fairleigh and walked away from her. He leaned against a wooden beam and slowly sunk to the ground. Crouched down, he began to cry again and covered his face in his hands. Fairleigh rushed over to comfort him.

"Fairleigh, I have a lot to tell you and the worst part is we can't be together again after I tell you. I never told you because

I knew you wouldn't have anything to do with me if I did and I loved you so much I couldn't bear the thought of not being with you every day. Fairleigh, I am the Prince of the Leprechauns."

Fairleigh gasped, her hand flew to her mouth and she took several steps backward until she ran into the pig pen gate. The pigs squealed noisily. "This is why they cursed me and put me in the hope chest, I'm the one who took their prince away. What will happen to me if they find out I'm back?"

"Well, right now they are trying to find me. They obviously don't know you are here. They sent who I thought was my loyal servant, Timothy Klein, to keep watch over you." At that announcement Bridget and Esther clutched each other. No wonder Timothy Klein was trying to reclaim the hope chest. He was a leprechaun. Connor stood up and approached Fairleigh who moved and kept backing up.

"Please Fairleigh, I love you and I would never hurt you. That's why I ran away. I fell in love with you and when I did, I began to see the evil ways of the leprechauns I tried to change them. They called me a traitor and tried to overpower me but my magic is more powerful and I got away. The problem is how to help you."

At the end of that sentence, Fairleigh who was leaning against another beam, also slid down the beam, collapsing. The two stared at each other from across the barn; sadness was heavy between them. Their eyes locked and immediately little colored stars traveled from Connor's eyes to Fairleigh's. The atmosphere changed from one of despair to one of intense love.

Esther and Bridget looked at one another, astonished, and slowly climbed down the loft. Suddenly Connor noticed them and jumped up. The stars stopped their path and immediately encircled Connor, followed by a large white star shaped like an arrow. The stars around Fairleigh did the same thing.

Connor cried, "Don't worry, Fairleigh, the stars will protect you. Now who in the bloody Irish world are you?"

Fairleigh ran over to the girls and stood in front of them. "Connor, it's o.k., these are my friends, Bridget and Esther. It is because of their help that I am here."

Connor relaxed, "Oh, so sorry, pleased to meet you. Thank you for helping me girl," he smiled and came to the girls, kissing their hands in greeting. Each girl felt the tremendous vibration of goodness come through his touch. They knew they could trust the Prince of Leprechauns. The girls giggled.

Fairleigh ran and closed the barn door and latched it. She came to Connor and pulled his hand and Bridget's, "We'll plot what to do. Now sit down crisscross applesauce." The four held hands and Connor, perplexed, tried to follow the girls. He found himself frustrated and just sat like a boy, hands locked around his raised knees.

He spoke first, "Now there isn't much time, I have to keep a step ahead of those leprechauns. I can't stay in one place for too long." Connor smiled, a request for the girls to continue. The stars that had been circling Connor and Fairleigh gently faded away.

Suddenly the barn door began to shake violently. A shrill

little Irish girlish voice screamed, "Let me in Prince Connor, I know you're in there!"

Connor jumped up. "Quick, girls, back up to the loft, hide." He lifted his hands as if to lift them up and a tremendous array of stars surrounded the girls like a cushion and lifted them faster than the blink of an eye into the hay loft.

No sooner had they landed than the door burst open and in came the tiny leprechaun who had served drinks at the gathering, followed by her maidservant. In a sparkly green taffeta dress, those upturned elfish shoes and a beautiful pewter crown with tiny emeralds, she was darling in an elfish sort of way. She was also green with envy. She stood with her tiny hands on her tiny hips.

Connor, also with hands on hips, was angry. "How did you find me, Caitlin, and did you tell the others?"

"Of course not, you know I wouldn't betray you." Her eyes traveled around the barn as she spoke. "Why did you lock the door? You aren't alone, are you?" She looked at Connor suspiciously. He was equally suspicious. "What about Kayla? You brought her along before and she betrayed us before." They both eyed Kayla threateningly.

The tiny maidservant, even smaller than Caitlin, bowed respectfully. "Prince Connor, they made me tell, they threatened to take me soul. Please forgive me, I won't say a word." She very worriedly backed up and ran into the barn door.

"The both of you must return and forget about me, stop following me," Connor was angry and as he and Caitlin faced off, stars began to fly between the two until Caitlin, exhausted, fell in a heap on the barn floor.

Connor looked down at her and spoke. "Caitlin, you know my magic is more powerful. You need to leave me alone."

Caitlin whispered, "Listen, Connor, they are on your trail. You had better give up and come back with me or you'll have to keep running for eternity. You know you don't want a life like that."

Connor stopped the star attack and began to pace the

barn floor. "Caitlin, it's my life and I want you to leave now. Thank you, but stop worrying about me. You'll only put yourself and your soul in danger." Connor took her by the shoulders and walked her towards the barn door. She argued with him as they walked. He slapped her on her bottom and sent her flying out the door with Kayla running fast behind.

Just then Esther sneezed in the hayloft. Connor stopped, breathless, hoping it wasn't heard. Bridget held her hand over Esther's mouth.

Of course, Caitlin heard it with those leprechaun ears! She was back in a flash, hands on hips again.

"Connor, don't even try to tell me that was you! Who are you hiding in here?" She pushed past him back into the barn, with stars lifting her she hovered above the hay loft and began madly throwing hay around, "Help me, Kayla."

Little Kayla rose with the stars and joined her mistress. Connor was yelling from below for them to stop when suddenly Kayla uncovered Esther and Caitlin uncovered Bridget. The girls stared in amazement at each other while Fairleigh quickly scampered down and hid behind Connor. The two slowly inched their way to the barn doors to escape when Caitlin screamed "Connor," and turned towards his direction. She immediately spied Fairleigh and dashed down and grabbed Fairleigh by the hair.

Connor grabbed Caitlin in turn by the hair and the three fought for all of three seconds until Connor had Caitlin firmly by the waist and held her in the air.

"Let go, Caitlin, before I do something we will both regret." With stars dashing out of his eyes, he surrounded the little leprechaun in a cage of stars. She hovered in the air with arms crossed, furious.

"Now there, you'll stay until I say so," Connor helped Fairleigh and smoothed her hair and wrinkled dress. Then Connor and Caitlin began to fight verbally in a celtic language that Bridget could not understand.

"Wait a minute," Esther whispered hysterically. "That's

Hebrew. They're speaking Hebrew!"

The letters began to fly all around their heads, white and sparkly and full of power. Esther pointed at each one and yelled out their names. As she did so, the letters suddenly seemed to jump to attention and soared up to the hay loft encircling Esther's head. Connor and Caitlin stopped quarreling and stared as the letters left them. This had never happened before. They stared up into the hay loft at Esther who had her hands in the air trying to touch them. They were elusive; they wouldn't let Esther touch them yet they wouldn't leave her.

"Esther, do you know the letters? Do you know how to use their combinations?" Connor yelled up, excited that he may have met someone who also knew their immense power. Suddenly everyone stopped dead. A thunderous noise came from outside the barn; little Kayla flew down to the doors and peered through the crack in the hinges, "They're coming! They're here, they've found the trail!" she jumped up and down frantically.

Connor pulled the stars from around Caitlin and held her

firmly by the shoulders, "If you've ever cared about me, stall them." He grabbed Fairleigh with one hand and Bridget with the other. Bridget grabbed Esther and they all ran out the barn door.

They were spotted. Dozens of leprechauns were screaming and shouting and trying to reach the barn. Caitlin held true to her feelings for Connor and raced back and forth with Kayla making a wall of stars in the beautiful meadow. It slowed down the leprechauns. They had to fight through them as though they were thistle bushes. As Connor's personal servants, they had been given special powers that regular leprechauns did not have. They were using them now, but they were only a temporary fix.

"We haven't much time," Connor yelled as they ran into the meadow and towards a green forest.

"But, Connor, where are we going? How can we ever escape them?" Bridget cried out breathlessly.

"To me rainbow," Connor yelled out, "me father always told me it was the only safe and private haven I had. He used to tell me if I had to think or meditate, it was the only place nobody could bother me. I never thought about using it because I was so happy spending time with Fairleigh." The two smiled at each other and Connor squeezed Fairleigh's hand tighter.

Chapter 8

"But Connor, is it safe from the leprechauns? Can't they come after us?" Fairleigh shouted, very worried.

"Not if what me father said was true," Connor did look a little worried. "We have to risk it though, we don't seem to have any other choices right now." It was hard to believe that in this forest there could be a rainbow. It was dense and dark and full of trees.

They kept running but Esther began to complain, "I'm tired, I have to rest; I'm not used to this." She fell down in a heap.

Connor stopped and waved his hands around Esther and the stars came out and followed his hands. He fashioned a sled made of stars and Esther leaned back in the hovercraft. Connor leaned over her and whispered, "If you can understand the code of the Hebrew letters you can take care of yourself. They still haven't left you. They have a magic of their own if your soul is bent on giving when you receive and your soul is good and always looking toward the white light," he smiled and grabbed the other girl's hands. The star cart with Esther followed close behind.

Esther couldn't take her eyes off the letters as they danced over her head. They seemed to have a personality all of their own. They appeared to woo her. She felt a wonderful warmth from the letters. She wanted to know them like people. They touched her soul in a comforting way. It was like getting to know someone for the first time that you thought you already knew.

"Connor, why don't you use your magic and whisk us all to the rainbow instead of all this running," Bridget couldn't understand why he didn't use his powers and just get them out of this mess. "Yes, why don't you?" Fairleigh chimed in.

Connor spoke as they ran. "It doesn't work that way. Things have changed since my father's emerald staff was taken from me by the leprechauns. With that I would have been able to create some magic but since it's gone I've developed my own powers. They were there before but not as strong.

"It is a little bit like becoming blind. Other senses become stronger than they were and that is what happened to my powers. The only thing is that they only work when things are desperate. I can feel a tingling sensation when I have the powers to use the stars. Then I know it's o.k. I can't and I won't abuse my powers or they'll leave. My powers are positive, they're good, not like the leprechauns which are evil. I don't want to be a part of that negative side. It isn't right."

Up ahead there was a circular clearing in the forest, beautiful soft grass enclosed it and in the middle was a beautiful colorful rainbow that went like a staircase from the meadow up through the trees to the sky. You couldn't even see where it ended. The little entourage stopped and stared. It was breathtakingly awesome. The multicolored rainbow colors were more brilliant than anything Bridget and Esther had ever seen. Against the dark forest and green grass it seemed almost unreal.

"Let's go," Connor excitedly led them over to the rainbow. He began to ascend it as though there were an invisible staircase inside of the rainbow. But the three girls stopped and he was yanked to a standstill while still holding their hands. "What's wrong? We have to hurry, this is our only chance, they'll catch up to us soon."

Connor looked puzzled at the girls who stood fearful. They hadn't seen stairs or anything and they couldn't understand how he was climbing. Also, it was extremely high; the rainbow went all the way into a cloud in the sky. Then it hit him, hard. He understood their fear. Even though time was of the essence he patiently took the time to explain.

"Ever since I was a young child, my father had drilled into me the faith and trust of God and the other side, that of which none of us can see or hear, feel or touch or taste with our five senses. That is how I access the power of the letters, by understanding there are other senses we have that are intangible, not of this world. Most of us don't believe what we can't comprehend with one of our senses. But you need to trust God, believe in the good side. There is nothing to fear but fear itself. I have been there, watching the leprechauns go to the negative side. But through the love of Fairleigh I came back to what I was taught as a lad. Believe me now girls, you all know you can trust me."

The girls looked at each other. They knew also that Connor was good. They would have to trust. Just then a tremendous racket was heard through the thick forest. Those leprechauns were coming! The girls leapt onto the rainbow which was like gliding into a cloud. The moment they stepped onto the cloud the leprechauns came hurling into the clearing. The little green men grabbed the end of the star cart and Esther's dress. Esther screamed.

Connor yelled down to Esther, "Esther use the letters,

they seem to know you, they still haven't left your side. They will help you if you are certain about them. Close your eyes and focus, it is your only chance," Connor looked worried and whispered to Fairleigh, "I can't help her, I don't have the tingling to use my stars. I know she can do it if she just believes." They all watched nervously as Esther clenched her eyes shut. The letters raced between Esther's feet and the leprechauns. As though lightning or electricity hit them, they pulled back in pain and the star cart with Esther dashed like a roller coaster up the rainbow and stopped at a dead jolt in front of Connor.

Connor hugged Esther and their eyes locked, "You did it, Esther! You believed past your five senses and you were protected. Let's go!" The foursome climbed higher and higher before they looked down again. When they did, they saw a wall of white light blocking the leprechauns from the rainbow.

Connor, a little out of breath stopped to explain, "It is the wall of good; and evil thoughts and people just can't penetrate through." They all stared as the leprechauns tried to push through the wall of light. Suddenly a small hand pushed through the wall of light, then a foot, then a mass of curls. It was Kayla, she had pushed through! Connor smiled with relief and that smile doubled as he saw Caitlin emerge as well. Connor shouted down laughingly at the two, "I didn't know the meaning of a faithful servant until just now." The two leapt into his arms and with one in each hand he swung them around the colorful rainbow with colors flying. The Hebrew letters left Esther and joined the celebration dancing amongst the three. Connor sang to the two tiny leprechauns:

> My friends, my pals, my servant maids;
>
> How can I thank you for your diligent ways?
>
> My true, my best, my darling Irish girls
>
> The letters have dissolved your evil days.

Everyone laughed and hugged, and Connor put them down with a pat on each of their heads.

"Let's go!" he shouted and grabbed Fairleigh's hand again and continued the climb up the beautiful rainbow. The two tiny leprechauns hovered over Connor's head. Birds of all kinds flew around them as they climbed higher and higher into the blue sky. Finally they reached what looked like that infamous pot of gold at the end of the rainbow.

Connor laughed and called to the letters. The huge pot was actually a golden door. One would never have known had they not seen it open. Connor laid both of his hands on the giant pot door and the letters danced around his head. The door opened and Connor stepped onto what was a field of golden grass. The moment he stepped onto it, a crown of green emeralds suddenly materialized on his head. It was breathtakingly beautiful. The girls gasped in astonishment. The letters continued to dance around Connor's head. He waved his arms as if beckoning someone over, and one at a time several white clouds came over and scooped each girl up.

Bridget laughed, "this is like my cozy club chair at home." Esther had her own treat with a little "k" in a circle, this was a kosher symbol. Esther laughed and held it up to Connor,

"How did you know?" Connor looked puzzled, "what are you talking about?"

Each chair had treats in the arms of the chairs. Each cloud chair also had a cup holder with beautiful clear mugs of hot white chocolate and a small plate of fruit and cookies. The girls were ravenously hungry.

"These are indescribably delicious," Bridget mumbled with her mouth full.

As they ate, the chairs began to move until the group was in a circle. Beautiful meditative music permeated the atmosphere. They knew they were safe. Connor was awestruck as well. "If this is a meditating room I need to see the water rooms...." Connor muttered to himself gazing around. There was so much his father had told him and he had thought he had forgotten. He was beginning to remember more clearly now what his father had told him about but he had never investigated. He vowed to explore what had been explained to him.

"Connor," Bridget began with her mouth still full of

cookies and her hands around the warm mug, "if you have never been here before, how did you know what to do with the clouds?" She was quite observant and noticed everything he was doing.

"Bridget, it may be hard for you to understand but information is channeled into my head from my guides or guardian angels. They tell me what to do and of course it is my choice whether to do it or not, but I have learned to trust them. We all have guides or angels around us. If we listen closely they will guide us. It is developed slowly, through meditation; it takes time, it won't happen immediately. But through consistent practicing, the messages will come."

Suddenly the girls were frozen like statues and Connor alone heard his father's voice.

"When you are ready the divine ways will penetrate your thoughts and desires. Now that you need them, and you are desirous of good and are ready to receive in order to share, they will come to you." Connor was shocked. His father had died many years ago, but now he heard his voice very clearly, only through his thoughts, not through a voice. But he sensed his real presence as if he was there talking to him; Connor was not imagining this. The girls looked like ice cubes.

His father continued, "the hope chest that kept your beloved Fairleigh is very powerful because it has been infused deeply over a long period of time with Fairleigh' s love and devotion and hopes for your future. Hopes and dreams are more powerful than most people realize. You must find it and put the American girls back inside it. It is their only way back to their lives. If they don't go back they may be unhappy here, especially the little Jewish girl. But I do believe Esther will benefit herself and her people if she takes some time before she returns to get to know her Hebrew letters in a way she never has.

"Now don't worry about the leprechauns. The rainbow will eventually dissolve and follow another rainstorm. When it dissolves it will disappear from the leprechauns' sight and gently deposit you and the girls in a meadow. Unfortunately, we don't know exactly where but you must find the hope chest.

"Good luck, my son, and may God be with you and your friends. Don't forget you have the stars and the letters to help you. Now you know that the rainbow is there for you following a rainstorm. Luckily we live in Ireland and there are many rainstorms with rainbows. They are so infrequent and inaccessible in other countries. Esther will be another help for you as soon as she believes completely in the letters. She has the abilities and the power because her soul is full of true goodness, but it is an added advantage that she is Jewish.

"In her time period she should know more about them than we do here, but obviously the people of the future ignored them and they were lost. Their society will only get worse if they don't grab onto the immense power and comfort the letters have."

With that last word Connor's father's voice stopped and the girls were unfrozen as though nothing had happened. Connor explained to the girls that the rainbow would soon dissolve and they would have to find the hope chest. He suggested they rest until then, since they would have another journey to find the hope chest. Everyone fidgeted in their couch chairs and finally closed their eyes and went to sleep. Esther was the last one; she couldn't stop staring at those letters dancing over her head. Connor smiled watching her.

"Esther, watch, I'll show you a combination." He pointed to the letters and called out three of them and they pulled out of the circle and stood at attention apart from the rest.

"But," Esther complained, "I know Hebrew and that doesn't make a real word."

"It's a code, silly. It helps you to think positively, just stare at it a moment. Haven't you ever played games with your own language like Pig Latin or made a club and had secret codes with English that looked like nonsense to everybody else?" Connor shut his eyes to take a nap. Esther stared a while and thought about what he said and fell asleep smiling. Those letters were comforting so far away from home.

Chapter 9

Suddenly the cloud chairs bounced down on another beautiful green meadow near a lake. There was a beautiful old castle nearby overlooking the lake and the meadow. The cloud chair landing was soft but bounced enough to wake them all up, but they all felt well rested. Everyone stretched and looked around, Ireland was so beautiful.

"I only hope we're far away from those leprechauns so we have some time to find the hope chest," Connor stood up looking a tad worried. The emerald crown was still on his head, glimmering brightly. It looked as though he were born with it on; it fit perfectly on his head and never even jostled when he moved.

"Thank goodness I know where we are," Connor looked

relieved.

"I know, we're on the outskirts of our village and that is the old Fitzgerald Castle," Fairleigh smiled, also relieved that the rainbow hadn't deposited them somewhere further away.

"Who lives there?" quipped Bridget, a little nervous.

"You sound like you are afraid it's a ghost," Fairleigh teased. "Nothing to worry about, a very old retired priest lives there. His name is Father Herman and he must be 101. His family was very wealthy and he had nothing to do with any of them his whole life. He thought they were too involved with money and things. But after everyone died and he was too old to be an active priest, he decided to retire there. He wanted to change the reputation of his family and use the money to do good. He is very kind. He uses the old castle to give poor people a place to live until they have enough money saved to buy their own farm."

"Let's go everybody. Fairleigh, lead us to the thicket where you hid the hope chest. Let's hurry, I have no idea where those leprechauns are," Connor began to walk quickly across the meadow with the two loyal leprechauns Caitlin and Kayla still hovering over his head. Suddenly they heard that nasty familiar green noise from behind; the leprechauns were raging behind them again.

"Oh no!" groaned Bridget and Esther.

"Quick, get into the lake, were going for a swim. The leps hate water," Connor yelled. "Get out on the other side and run to the castle. Father Herman will have none of their nonsense. The problem is getting back out of the castle. We'll have to make another plan inside."

Esther complained, " I can't swim very well and I have a dress on. Is it deep, is there anything dangerous in there?"

Connor stopped at a dead jolt at the water's edge and everyone ran into him and tumbled back on the grass. They couldn't help but giggle at the whole mess! He cautiously put one toe out on what looked like a rock and stepped on it, then he noticed another one and put the other foot on it. He was on the lake looking like he was walking on water! He smiled as he saw another and another, "Esther, your hopes were answered! Come on everybody follow me, it's a wonderful coincidence!" They all held hands and slowly walked across the lake on the stones.

"There is no such thing as a coincidence," Esther whispered loudly to Bridget.

"I heard that," Connor laughed at the head of the line. "You are right, Esther, it is a miracle, God is on our side."

The group was in the middle of the lake when Esther stopped to glance over her shoulder. She was very worried the leprechauns would follow them and they'd be fighting in the middle of the lake. She was last in the line and sure she would be first to be grabbed. Behind her all the leprechauns were on the edge of the lake screaming and pointing in amazement. Esther was sure they would see the stones at any moment and come hurling across. Then she looked down at the last stone she had stepped on, but it was not there! She looked further, none of the stones were there! Only the ones in front of her were there!

"Hurry everybody, the stones are sinking," she screamed.

Connor turned around to look and everyone stopped. "Esther, stand still for a moment, fear of fear is what is frightening you. They won't sink for us, they are protecting us.'"

He called out to three of the letters and they floated over to Esther's head.

Esther muttered under her breath, "that's not a word." Connor heard her and reminded her, "It's a code, Esther, that one is for protection. Belief is all we need."

Esther stared as the letters floated over her head. She felt protected. She knew in her heart she was protected. Her soul had been touched. Here was an aspect of her Jewishness she knew nothing about but she knew she had to learn more and trust senses that were not of the five earthly ones. It was fascinating and wonderful and she wanted to learn more.

Bridget squeezed her hand tightly, "we have to have hope Esther, have hope!"

"But, Connor, it is still scary with those leprechauns after us," Esther remained frightened.

"I know," Connor's voice was comforting. "That is life. But when your faith is strong you will be protected. Be certain and you will be fine. Hope still has some doubt in it, be certain!" He was interrupted by a scream from Fairleigh. "Look, the leprechauns are running around the lake--hurry, run!" Holding hands they all ran across the stones to the other side. "Quick, run to the castle, the leprechauns will never dare to cross into the priest's home."

The castle was old and the moat had scummy green mold in the water. The moat surrounded the castle with a rickety drawbridge lying down over it. The chains were rusty and it looked doubtful it would go up to keep the leps from crossing over. Bridget, although scared, was also thrilled at seeing an authentic stone castle, moat and drawbridge after reading about them so often.

They all ran across the drawbridge. Esther tripped and fell down unconscious. Quicker than the blink of an eye, a green arm grabbed her. The leps all ran off with their prisoner.

Bridget reached behind to grab Esther's hand for the

drawbridge was rickety. When she realized Esther had not taken her hand, she turned around and saw several leprechauns carrying her off. Esther had come to and was screaming and yelling and struggling to get away but there were too many of those little green men hanging on to her.

Bridget screamed and the rest of the group turned to see poor Esther being carried off.

Connor jumped off the drawbridge and turned to the group, "everybody stay here, I can't risk any more of you being kidnapped; now I mean it!" Connor's voice had changed drastically. It was loud and firm in a voice like a powerful, older king, a voice no one dared disobey, a voice they trusted and respected and they stopped in their tracks. Connor ran off after Esther.

The Hope Chest

Chapter 10

As Connor ran after the leps and Esther, the group watched in horror and then amazement, for suddenly, Connor disappeared. It was as though he turned invisible.

Connor in fact, had turned invisible. As he ran he had taken off his beautiful emerald studded belt and put it back on inside out, which made him invisible the moment he rebuckled it in this position.

Meanwhile, back at the castle, the group stood in shock. A resounding old voice hollered out, "what in the bloody world is going on out here?" Father Herman suddenly appeared. Very tall and thin in black robes and a round beanie hat that Bridget thought looked like a Jewish yomica, with silver bushy eyebrows to match, the old priest stood with his hands on his hips. There was a familiarity to him that Bridget thought reminded her of Father Bailey. He had a wonderful air about him and Bridget was hopeful he could help them find Esther and Connor. Fairleigh ran to him and hugged him and started babbling. He chuckled as he ushered them all into the castle.

Connor ran after the leps faster than lightning. He finally caught up with them fairly deep in the forest.

Apparently Esther was unconscious or drugged or under a spell, as he heard nothing and couldn't see Esther. They must still be carrying her, he thought to himself.

Suddenly he spied the group and Esther's curls dangling from the middle of their green huddle. About six leps were carrying her. They approached two large trees in the forest approximately three feet apart from each other. Each leprechaun walked backwards into the space between the two trees with their right arm curved into their side to form a circle and their tongues sticking out and eyes closed. In the middle of the space they jumped up about twenty feet and into an opening in the trunk of the tree that suddenly appeared on the right then they disappeared.

Connor was very familiar with this secret body code to enter the land of the leprechauns. As soon as they entered they disappeared. The land of the leprechauns was invisible to the human eye; it existed in another dimension. Even though Connor was invisible, he still had to do it to get inside. Connor quickly went through the motions and immediately was in his homeland. The familiar atmosphere was cool and murky. It was a huge cave bigger than any building in an American city, even the Empire State Building.

It had green moss dripping over the walls like a strange wallpaper that hung from the ceiling like icicles in an igloo. There was a large lake in the middle of the cave with green bubbling water. Steam was so thick over it from the heat that it looked like a fog hovered over the top of the water. Soft green grass covered the ground and wilting plants and flowers made for a sad feel to the place. Leprechauns were everywhere, pushing wheelbarrows made of gold, full of giant pale green mushrooms; their favorite food. The place looked terrible. Connor was horrified. The leps had abandoned their beautiful gardening abilities. Connor's home was a mess: cold, ugly and not kept up like it used to be. The transformation of the leps was also evident in their home, their land and their nasty new evil ways. Connor was very saddened.

The light was creepy with lots of giant candles everywhere, but their glow was tiny and sad and barely a flame flickered from them. It was the only source of warmth in the massive, cold damp cave. Spooky soft music came from a harpist playing in a nook high up on the cave wall. All leps could play the harp and they took shifts. They either jumped or climbed the mossy, ropey vines to get up to the music loft. They all had frowns and miserable looks on their faces. Long gone were the cheerful smiles Connor remembered. The whole place had a sad, negative feeling. The days of the cheerful cave were gone. Connor trembled looking at the awful sight.

He quickly spied the leps that were carrying Esther. They approached the lake and pulled a round saucer-shaped boat hammered from gold and filled with soft moss off the shore. It was one of the last remnants of cheerful times in the cave. The leps placed Esther inside, still groggy but beginning to stir. They said, "be still or you'll boil like an egg!" and with that they pushed her off to the middle of the lake. With the shove Esther awoke completely and began screaming. Her curls bounced with her screams and the boat rocked frantically.

One of the leps picked up a conical cone-shaped snail and asked the snail to leave the shell for a minute. The slug scurried off to hide under a leafy green wilting plant and the lep bellowed through the snail shell which amplified his voice like a microphone. "You there with the bouncy hair, you might be interested to know if you tip that boat you'll boil so quickly we'll be able to spoon you into a bread pudding!" He laughed and gave the shell back to the hiding slug who crawled in faster than the speed of light.

Esther quickly realized how hot the water was and settled down, tears still streaming down her face.

Connor pondered what to do. He sat down on a giant mushroom with both hands on his cheeks. First, he had to calm down from the shock of the boiling water in the lake, which had always been a pleasant cool temperature. The misery of his home and the negativity in the atmosphere put Connor in a sad mood, but he knew he had to remain hopeful.

Even if he could get to Esther in the middle of the lake and bring her to shore, they would be after her immediately. He couldn't make her invisible.

Connor slid down the mushroom and leaned against it. He closed his eyes to think and to meditate. After a while he scrunched his eyes and rubbed his forehead. He tried to sift through all the wisdom his father had taught him. Suddenly a thought entered his mind from one of his conversations with his father, "sometimes, son, being upside down has its advantages."

Connor looked puzzled, why would that thought enter his

mind? He knew he had to go with it. That was one of his father's often repeated reminders; go with what falls out of the sky, there is always a reason that thought or idea came your way. Being upside down has its advantages. Suddenly he remembered a time a very long time ago. He was only a little boy, about seven-or eight-years old. He closed his eyes and flashed back. He was in the middle of the lake on a saucer boat with his father. Everything was beautiful, lush, green, bright white light, gorgeous flowers and plants. The water was the perfect temperature to swim in.

One of the leprechaun servants had yelled from the shore to his father in a very irritated and annoyed manner. His father quickly and authoritatively reprimanded the servant who sulked off. As soon as he had disappeared, his father whispered to him, "If you are ever confronted by a traitor or an enemy that penetrates here, go over the boat backwards and upside down. It will appear as if you had toppled over and drowned by the depths of the lake. For if you dive in, they will certainly guess there is somewhere you are going or that you are trying to escape.

Of course the water in those times was never boiling, but perfect for swimming and full of beautiful talking fish. These fish, his father told him, would cover his mouth with theirs and give him oxygen. Connor worried how those fish could be alive in that boiling water though. The fish were also entertaining and spiritual. If a leprechaun child performed a good deed or a "mitzvah" in leprechaun language, the child would report the deed to the fish and the fish would perform. This is one of the main ways that lep children were brought up to do good, it was an incredible reward. It was a joy to watch the colorful fish singing and jumping. Adult leprechauns could do this too, but they usually reserved the pleasure for the children.

Connor trembled at the thought of those beautiful fish being boiled to death. What had happened to these leprechauns? They were so evil and nasty now. It was as if they had all been brainwashed.

He pondered what lay beneath the lake. He figured there was some sort of escape tunnel or hatch, but he wasn't sure.

Also, the water was beautiful then, but now it was boiling. What could he do? He thought he had better get over to Esther and at least calm her down.

He retrieved a saucer boat from the edge of the water, hoping anyone who saw it would just think it drifted off. He pulled some dead branches in with him to act as oars if need be. Connor got in and pushed off the shore with his foot as hard as he could. Suddenly a little tiny green hand grabbed the saucer. It was a lep child who had been playing behind a mushroom. Connor shoved him off gently. The child had no idea what had just happened and ran off crying to his mommy.

Nobody seemed to notice much wrong so he took a branch with lots of twigs and leaves and paddled towards Esther.

"Esther, grab my boat. It's me Connor, I'm invisible."

Esther gave a little gasp of surprise and grabbed the edge of the saucer. "Oh Connor, thank God you are here, I'm so scared."

"Esther, listen to me. I think there's an escape hatch in

the middle of the lake…." and he explained the whole story from when he was little and what his father had told him.

"But Esther," Connor breathlessly finished up, "we still have the problem of the boiling lake water."

They both sat there pondering. Esther, shivering in fear, put her hands in her sweater pockets and pulled them out gasping and stammering in excitement.

Chapter 11

"Connor, I completely forgot, look, wishing glue!" Fairleigh made me and Bridget put some in our pockets from the hope chest. All we have to do is rub it on ourselves and wish protection from the boiling lake!"

"Esther, this is wonderful!" Connor kissed her hand and Esther blushed. She gave Connor a blob of the glue and they rubbed it all over themselves.

"Esther, now listen, you have to tumble out of the boat and backwards, head first like you're upside down, a headstand, o.k.? We'll do it together, are you ready?"

Connor took Esther's hand and over the boat they tumbled into the boiling lake waters. Some leps on the shore heard the crash and brought the leaders running.

"She couldn't take it, she did herself in," they mumbled shaking their heads.

Meanwhile under the water Connor and Esther tumbled with water boiling all around them within an inch of their bodies. But the boiling water never touched them and they could breathe comfortably. Almost immediately they saw at the bottom of the lake a statue of Connor's father with outstretched arms and hands. Connor and Esther each instinctively grabbed a hand and were instantly sucked into a tunnel at the foot of the statue. The water was immediately pushed out and they were dry and able to breathe. They collected themselves and began to walk through the tunnel. Obviously it had not been used in a terribly long time. There were massive spider webs everywhere.

Esther was so worried, she sighed every once in a while. Connor took her hand and placed it through his elbow as they trudged through the tunnel. Connor tried to cheer her up.

"Hey Esther, have you ever played with spider webs in leprechaun land?" Connor reached up to one on the tunnel wall and rolled it up into a ball and began bouncing it around. Esther smiled. Connor looked like an American boy back home playing basketball with the spider web ball. He jumped and threw it to Esther as they made their way down the passage way.

Suddenly, part of the tunnel wall burst open and they were confronted by another leprechaun. He was a teenage lep and looked very nervous. Apparently there was a door on the other side that was not visible on the tunnel side.

Connor quickly jumped in front of Esther to protect her and slid the spider web ball into her sweater pocket.

The lep cried out, "Who are you, intruder?" Connor was still invisible and the lep could only see Esther. He pulled a whistle out of his pocket, that looked like a little flute and he played it like one. But Connor knew it was loud and piercing and grabbed it from the lep before he could blow it. The lep looked at Esther in surprise.

"What kind of magician are you?"

Connor came up behind him and waved his arms all

around him like he was tying him up with rope. He was tying him up, with stars in fact. The stars bound him up well; Connor even popped one in his mouth to keep him quiet.

Connor grabbed Esther's hand and they ran down through the tunnel.

Suddenly Esther tripped, luckily she was hanging onto Connor's elbow and he kept her from falling. She gasped as she straightened up.

"Look Connor, look what I tripped on," she pointed to a large lizard on the mossy tunnel floor. It looked just like the mossy floor. Connor bent down to look at it and the lizard stared right back at Connor.

"Esther, it's a chameleon, do you know what that is?"

"Sure Connor, it's a reptile that changes its color to blend in with its environment."

"Yes Esther, but with one difference, remember you are in leprechaun land. If you hold it, you will also change color. Pick it up, and it will help me get you out of here." Esther picked up the chameleon which took a long blink and smiled a lazy smile. It was a friendly creature but big and difficult to hold.

Connor took it out of her hands and placed it on her shoulder, and draped the chameleon around her neck, sort of like a shawl. Connor chuckled, Esther giggled and the chameleon yawned. Almost immediately Esther turned the colors of the tunnel.

"Perfect!" Connor smiled, "This is almost as good as being invisible." He and Esther continued down through the tunnel.

Suddenly another portion of the wall opened and more leps came through. They had nasty, angry looks on their faces. They were mean and grumbly as they looked all around them, obviously looking for their missing comrade. They stared right through Connor and Esther and shrugged their shoulders.

They disappeared and Connor cried out, "Fabulous! It worked--they didn't see you!" As soon as they left Connor went to the tunnel wall and tried to open the area where they came out of but he couldn't figure it out. He shrugged his shoulders and they trudged on. Connor and Esther continued, with Connor being completely invisible and Esther cloaked in an array of colors produced from the protection of the chameleon.

Soon they spotted an opening. Connor peered in and then told Esther to wait while he investigated. In the damp cave was a hovering green fog with eerie music penetrating the walls. It was cold and damp and you could feel it through to your bones. Connor knew this was the cave that Fairleigh was brought to. It was here they put her under a spell. He ran out quickly.

"Sorry Esther, it is just a dead end." He didn't want to worry her. He took her hand and they kept on. After what seemed like a couple of miles they reached another dead end.

It looked like the end of the tunnel. The wall was thick and mossy and the plants growing out of it were very old. Connor felt the wall up and down with his hands, not knowing what he was looking for. Esther slumped down against the wall into a tired heap on the floor. She was ready to cry.

"Connor what do we do now? How are we going to get out of here?" she covered her face with her hands. Connor slid his back down the wall just as Esther had and rubbed his tired dusty eyes.

"Think, Connor, think," he mumbled over and over to himself. He began pounding the ground with his fists over and over in frustration and anger. He was still mumbling to himself. Esther started to giggle listening to the invisible Connor and joined him pounding her fists on the soft mossy ground believing she was mimicking him, "think, Connor, think." It actually was a good release of all the frustration and fear she had been feeling.

Suddenly the ground began to tremble and mounds of earth slowly bubbled up like water bubbling up out of a fountain. Just then, the round brown heads of several giant earthworms the size of Connor and Esther shot out of the holes they made in the earth!

One earthworm, slightly gray like the color of hair on a grandpa, with many wrinkles and small spectacles, spoke in a very distinguished voice.

"You called, Prince Connor? It's good to see you, I haven't seen you since you were a wee boy…" The elder worm turned his head this way and that as he spoke looking for the invisible Prince. "I know you are here but I can't see you, lad." As he went to adjust his spectacles, Connor quickly pulled his belt out, turned it around and put it back in, and instantly was visible again.

Esther, meanwhile, gently lifted the chameleon off of her shoulder and put it on the ground. The earthworms gently eyed her and chuckled a little. But as soon as Connor was visible, they bowed their heads deeply to the now visible prince.

"I always thought you were part of my dreams, I had no idea you were real." Connor went over to the elder worm and got down on one knee to be at eye level with the giant earthworm who stood in the shape of an L. Half of the length of his body lay on the ground like a snake and the other half rose into the air trying to meet the eyes of Connor. He appreciated the gesture of

Connor to meet him at eye level.

"Sometimes memories of childhood do seem like dreams," the giant spectacled worm replied.

Suddenly that familiar thunderous noise of many leps could be heard in the distance. "They're coming again Connor," Esther squealed and stooped down to scoop up the chameleon and held it around her neck. It was now a comfort, like a stuffed animal, to her.

"Hop on our backs," the earthworms came higher out of the ground so Esther and Connor could wrap themselves around their backs. As soon as they had wrapped their arms and legs around the bodies of the worms, they leapt completely out of the ground and into the air, diving head first back into the holes they had come out of. Dirt flew everywhere as the earthworms practically flew, or "squiggled" at a very high speed through the rich soil.

Chapter 12

Esther hung on for dear life as the worms were slippery but they had lots of ridges and wrinkles. Esther dug her hands and feet firmly into the ridges and felt pretty secure. It reminded her of a roller coaster ride, then she was able to enjoy this worm ride! Dirt flew over her head, never into her face or eyes so she soon unsqueezed them and began to see a whole new world, the earth underground. It was fascinating. They passed ant hills and beetle caves and she was amazed how the worms went around these homes and never collided with another insect. They came very close, but no accidents! They had amazing radar.

The smell of the rich soil was wonderful, clean, earthy and fresh. It brought memories of gardening with her mother in their lush backyard. She soon got tired and relaxed and closed her eyes to just enjoy the smell and the swishing of dirt as the worms tunneled rapidly through.

Connor spoke the entire journey with the elder worm on whose back he was squiggling on. Like Esther, Connor comfortably wedged his hands and feet into the deep wrinkles of the worm. He whispered into the worms hidden ears, "Thank you, you saved us. Can you get us safely back into the earthly forest so we can find our friends?"

"Of course, Prince Connor," your wish is our command. "I am so glad you somehow remembered how to call on us for help!"

Connor smiled as he had no idea banging his fists on the ground over and over would bring such a wonderful rescue squad. "But please take us far from the entrance to the leprechaun cave so we don't get attacked again."

"Where exactly do you need to go?" the worm asked.

"We need to get to Father Herman's castle on the earth side, do you know of it?"

"I know the tunnels around the moat very well. It is there we shall take you directly."

Connor breathed a sigh of relief and relaxed a moment and began to take in the sights around him as the worms tunneled swiftly through the rich soil. "Sir Worm, what is your name and how do you know me from my childhood?"

"I am Sir Berndt, known to the worms as Uncle Berndt and to your highnesses as Sir Berndt. I and my loyal worms are known as the foundation of the leprechaun community. But I answer only to your father, and since his death I now answer only to you.

"Since his death I have been very worried as I have heard of the turmoil and tyranny amongst the leps. An evil one has brainwashed the leprechaun community. I am so glad to have found you as you are now in command and I answer only to you since your father has passed on. Please remember we remain silent and only communicate with you. You remembered how to summon me and with that I am so pleased."

"No Sir Berndt, I did not remember, it was a coincidence," Connor said.

"Remember Prince Connor what your father told you and what the Zohar says, there is no coincidence. Pounding the ground and calling out your name summons me and tells me who needs me. But remember it only works for the immediate royal family. The leps are not aware of our capabilities. We are the secret army of your father and now we respond only to you. We are at your service, your highness."

Connor blushed as he was a modest, kind prince and didn't take to power easily. He hugged Sir Berndt and said, "please tell me of the days I've forgotten and tell me what is the meaning of your name?"

Sir Berndt smiled and a warmth filled his heart that in turn warmed his whole worm body. The worm's deep intuition told him that the Prince was of the same soul as his father. He was relieved to have made contact with him and established a relationship with King Connor. He knew the Prince was now

King but he knew Connor would not realize it until he resolved the issue with the traitors, the leps, and married and established a new kingdom.

Sir Berndt filled the rest of the journey with tales long forgotten of Connor when he was but a baby, and his father from when he was a lad.

Esther seemed to be enjoying her ride on the back of her worm behind Connor.

"Sir Berndt, do you know if the beautiful singing fish perished in the boiling lake?" Connor winced as he asked the wise worm.

"Don't worry, Prince Connor, we siphoned them through a tunnel to a deep underground well. When you have time, summon me again and I will take you to them."

Connor breathed a deep sigh and a tear rolled down his cheek.

"Thank you, Sir Brendt, I am deeply grateful. I love those fish."

The huge worm smiled warmly.

Soon the worms tunneled upwards and emerged through mud and there they were finally at the moat!

Connor and Esther scrambled off with just a few flecks of mud in their hair and clothes. They graciously bowed and thanked the worms.

"But Sir Berndt, you didn't tell me the meaning of your name." Connor was so interested and curious.

"Prince Connor, I gained my position and title through a contest where I burrowed my tunneling trails and skills faster than most worms. I left a trail of smoke behind me, which is next to impossible in this rich moist soil. They said I burn my tunnels I go so fast, hence I am Sir Berndt."

The loyal worm bowed deeply to the Prince and nodded to the other worms. They all shot out of the earth like arrows and dove in unison back into the tunnels of the earth.

Esther and Connor hugged each other and ran to the castle drawbridge shouting to everyone to let them in.

Chapter 13

Soon they were safely at the doorway of the huge old castle hugging and kissing their worried friends.

Father Herman beckoned them into the castle. "Come on in and rest your weary bones and do tell me what happened to you. Fairleigh and her friend have told me about the chase. I do love a good chase now and then," he chuckled.

Walking further into the castle, he motioned with his large hands for them to follow. With sighs of relief they walked into the largest circular foyer that Esther had ever seen. It was made of large round white stones, and the ceilings went up to the sky with a stained glass skylight of blue and white at the very top.

Art surrounded the round foyer with huge paintings

larger than life of old noble ladies and gentlemen. The priest walked through the foyer into a massive parlor. Huge fireplaces on either side of the gigantic room were surrounded with large comfy chairs and couches. Bridget was delighted with all the antique furniture. She whispered to Esther, "Isn't it beautiful? Wait until you see the rest of it!" She was wishing her mother could see this place.

The priest sat down on an enormous old dark wood, intricately carved chair upholstered in a dark green velvet; it resembled a throne. It looked well worn.

Obviously it was his favorite. He picked up some spectacles, took a moment to wind them around each ear, and peered at each person intently. He looked at Fairleigh, "Didn't you want to marry him? If my eyes aren't failing me, he's quite handsome and kinder than twice his looks."

"Oh, Father, I do still want to marry him but right now we can't stop running from those confounded leps!" Fairleigh began to cry and the priest rested his hands on her head as she lay her head on his knees. He stroked her beautiful red hair and reassured her.

"Fairleigh, I will do everything I can to help you. I need to think and I need the help of Connor, Caitlin and Kayla. Come here, wee ones, we need to talk." He motioned the little maiden leps from over Connor's head to come over to him. Father Herman handed Fairleigh a handkerchief and she went to sit with Connor. The two little leps hovered at the old priest's eye level. "Please Fairleigh, take your friends and show Esther the castle while I have a chat here with Connor." He waved them off.

"Connor, I know you have been through an ordeal but we need to move quickly to get ahead of them. They will be back, you know." He winked at the two little leps as he poured cups of tea at the little table beside his old throne. They winked back and two of the tea cups shrunk to their size. They each daintily took a cup of tea and each one got comfy on the knees of the old priest.

"Now then, let's have this out. I think we can find a

solution to this, don't you?" They all sipped their tea and then Father Herman said, "Do tell me what the leps are afraid of and don't even think of lying to me because you know I know. I just need a tiny confirmation." The priest thrust out his chin and took another sip of tea, staring strongly at each tiny lep. The two girls looked at each other and then at the priest with their tiny heads bowed low in shame.

Caitlin began, "Father, they are afraid of a queen. If Connor marries Fairleigh they know they must obey her and they are scared. They also are frightened of the fact that Connor has changed to the good side. They don't like it and want to continue to be selfish. They don't see the good in sharing and kindness; they think they will lose everything by being generous."

Caitlin bowed her head even lower until Father Herman had to lift her head out of her tiny cup of tea with his pinky finger.

He chuckled, "I knew it. But let me correct you. Not IF Connor marries Fairleigh but WHEN; however the most important thing is that they don't realize they will love Fairleigh as much as they love Connor. Fairleigh is an angel. She would never take advantage of them."

"But Father," Kayla interrupted, "Connor changed, completely and drastically and they think it is horrible and wrong and evil."

Connor interrupted and told them what the elder earthworm had said about the leps being brainwashed. He looked toward Kayla and Caitlin and said, "I need you two to tell me who was brainwashed and why you weren't, and what happened."

"Now Kayla," Father Herman gently patted her head with his index finger, "Connor has acknowledged nothing but goodness, Godliness, light and love. They will see this. They are only afraid of what they do not know. Now listen to Connor and tell us what you remember." He bowed his head low in anticipation of their story. Connor leaned forward and the lep girls began to whisper.

Meanwhile Fairleigh was giving an incredulous Esther a tour of the amazing old castle. There was a ballroom, a library with books up to the ceiling complete with ladders that slid along the walls! Lots and lots of bedrooms, all with fireplaces and beautifully adorned with antiques and linens. There was a gigantic kitchen, parlors and salons. All kinds of friendly people were cooking, cleaning, and taking care of the castle. Fairleigh explained that these people were receiving room and board by helping the priest cook, clean and maintain the huge castle and all its occupants until they were able to venture out on their own.

An hour later and still not through the castle tour, Connor appeared and interrupted, "Now, the most amazing part of the castle--the rooftop garden." Connor's eyes shone, he had hope now and a plan was in the making.

Through a winding staircase tower Connor led them to the top of the castle, onto an immense roof. The girls were awestruck. They thought they were back up in the sky. You could see all of Ireland and beyond. There were lush plants everywhere and old fashioned wicker patio furniture, pots of vegetable plants and water fountains.

It was lovely. Esther spied a tiny rainbow in one of the fountains and sat on the edge, mesmerized by it and remembering her experience in the rainbow. Connor came over and sat beside her. He whispered gently to Esther, "Focus now, make it bigger. Be positive and call on these three letters."

He called out three Hebrew letters. Esther smiled at his Irish accent pronouncing the oh-so-familiar Hebrew she had only heard from the mouth of the Rabbi at home. Beautiful music adorned with bells permeated the air as she whispered back each of the letters to Connor. The letters hovered adoringly and the tingling sensation Connor had described shivered through her body. It felt so comforting, so real and so true.

The rainbow got bigger and bigger until it filled the water of the fountain. She had never seen a rainbow under water. It was mesmerizing and seemed to dance under the water like a fish. It spoke to her heart. It told her only she had control of her life and the power of the letters would help her do good.

She smiled at Connor and whispered a teary thank you. "Connor, I wish it could take me home." Connor squeezed her shoulder.

"Me too, but unfortunately it's only local transportation." The two laughed. "But look, Esther, look what you made happen," and he shook her hand strongly in both of his.

"Connor, at home kids do high five," and she showed him the slap-your-hand greeting American kids do. The rainbow dissolved as they spoke and the priest emerged onto the roof.

"I think I have more of our plan ironed out," the old priest declared with a big grin on his face. Caitlin and Kayla sat on each of his shoulders. "But first I would like to do something a wee bit out of the ordinary." He walked towards Fairleigh and took her hand and then towards Connor and took his hand. He placed them together inside of his own large hands.

"I would like to ask the two of you to be married. Now I know ordinarily a man asks for the hand of his bride, but I know you two have been betrothed for an eternity. I know you both love each other and I know you are right for each other because I know you so well. Your marriage will help break the power of the nonsense with these here leprechauns."

Those little colored stars shot between the eyes of Fairleigh and Connor and the intense love between the two of them filled the roof like a warm breeze on an Irish summer day. They both said, "Yes," simultaneously and embraced each other and then Father Herman.

Laughing his hearty laugh, Father Herman pulled them apart, "Fairleigh take your girlfriends and go to me attic. Me mother's wedding dress has been sad up there since I became a priest. Try it on and come back here."

Connor was all smiles, "Father Herman, I can't thank you enough. This is what we both want so much. Now we can begin our lives together." He hugged the old priest.

"Now listen, Connor, come and sit. I need to talk to you. There's more to this day than your marriage." The priest pulled

Connor to a wicker bench and they sat there quietly talking.

Chapter 14

Fairleigh led the girls back into the castle where they made their way up to the attic. It was amazing, huge and spacious with lots of cobwebs, of course, and lots of old furniture. There were old books piled up high with dust, antique Tiffany lamps with beautiful stained glass, and to Bridget's delight, not one, but several antiquated beautiful hope chests. They were not quite like hers but absolutely beautiful, and each one was different. They were scattered amongst the attic and Bridget and Esther ran around counting them.

"Here's one," Esther shouted.

"Here's another one," Bridget called in delight. They continued this great counting game calling out another number as each girl spied one. Fairleigh laughed watching them and then busily began searching for the wedding dress, meanwhile humming in her sweet Irish lilting voice, "I'm going to be wed to my sweet Irishman Connor, my love, my groom.

"I called him a prince because he was kind,

And our hearts became intertwined

Little I knew he was really a prince

Till I got home and saw the crown on his head

Jewels of emeralds, our country's stone

They caused him to be a prisoner when he should be the leader

Now I must be his helper to regain his place, among the leprechauns

They must not fight."

"Girls, I need help, start looking in those hope chests for the gown, please," Fairleigh was getting frustrated looking at the dozen chests sprinkled around the room.

All three girls began tackling the contents of the hope chests.

"Fairleigh, these dresses are just beautiful. Do you think Father Herman would mind if we wore one for your wedding?" Bridget asked hopefully clutching a lovely linen dress.

"How could he mind if my bridesmaids had nothing else to wear?" Fairleigh exclaimed.

"Oh, Fairleigh!" both girls exclaimed at the same time and ran to hug her. "I've never been a bridesmaid before." Esther was delighted. In fact Bridget had never seen her so happy.

"But first we need to find that wedding gown," Fairleigh continued to tumble clothes out of the chests.

"Wait Fairleigh," Esther paused very quietly, "I'm getting an instinct rush like nothing back home. Stop, both of you and be very still." Suddenly a few of the Hebrew letters appeared and floated over an area in the far corner of the attic. They seemed to be pointing to what lay beneath them.

"Do you see them?" Esther whispered loudly.

"No," Fairleigh shook her head and Bridget just kept looking all around the attic turning in circles. Esther ran to the corner followed by Fairleigh and Bridget, and together they pulled off a heavy rug and a small table. Underneath the pile was yet another hope chest. All three gasped. It was very similar to Fairleigh and Bridget's hope chest. But instead of carved gardens there were scenes of carved animals and the feet were that of a lion's. They tried to open it but it was locked.

"Wait, I still have the key to Fairleigh's chest, let's try it out," Bridget pulled the key from her pocket and it fit perfectly into the lock! The lid opened all by itself and light emanated from within. The three gasped again and Fairleigh reached inside pulling out a large bundle. It was the wedding dress, untouched by time, exquisite as though it had just been purchased from a store (although it had to be older than Father Herman who was at least 101).

"Well, Esther, I guess you don't have to explain your 'instinct rush' and thank you. Connor was right about you. You must practice with the letters. You will be so pleased at what you can accomplish to help others and especially your family."

Fairleigh spoke as she unfolded the gorgeous gown. "You will also help yourself as you help others with your abilities. Look, if it wasn't for your desire to help me and your gift of the instinct rush we would never have found the dress," Fairleigh said as she held it up. It was a dream.

"Girls, can you help me get the dress on?" Fairleigh patted Bridget's arm, and Bridget and Esther unfastened all the buttons, hooks and eyes on the old-fashioned dress.

Fairleigh's face suddenly turned white. "Look girls," she whispered and pointed to a button at the bottom of the train of the dress. It was a twin to the button Fairleigh had found on her own dress. She sat down on the attic floor in a slump.

"What could this possibly mean?" She held it up and the girls all looked at it. Only a wise woman would have noticed it in the first place. It was just like all the rest, yet the bottom and edges were like the one on Fairleigh's dress, made of glass.

"I think the leps were trying to hold the priest's mother under a spell." Bridget pondered scratching her head. "But of course, a girl only wears a wedding dress once."

"You never took your dress off in the hope chest." Bridget wondered some more. Then to Esther who was rummaging through the attic making quite a racket, "Esther, what are you doing?"

"I saw a sewing basket somewhere over here. I have an idea, oh, here it is." Esther brought the sewing basket to the dress. While she removed a button from the neckline and began sewing it where the leprechaunic button was, she talked.

"Listen Fairleigh, wear your hair down so it covers this missing button. Everyone sees the train and it will look bad if a button is missing down here. You certainly can't wear the dress with the lep button on it. Now it won't look so bad." She quickly tied it off and the girls helped Fairleigh in. It was stunning and fit perfectly. Fairleigh was positively glowing with happiness.

While Bridget and Fairleigh fussed with the dress, Esther went over to the magnificent hope chest and walked around it several times and eventually stuck her head deep inside. "Bridge," a muffled Esther startled Bridget and Fairleigh and they came rushing over and pulled her out. "Bridge, do you think this hope chest could take us home? Try the key!" Sure enough there was a lock on the inside like the other chest but nothing happened with the key on the inside like the other chest.

"Begorra, girls, the other one is enchanted," Fairleigh said, matter of factly, using an Irish expression.

"But then why was this one emanating such a light?" Esther asked with her face in a thoughtful far away look.

"I don't know," Fairleigh said. "Let's ask Connor about it later."

Bridget and Esther found some beautiful white linen dresses, shoes and slips and underthings, all lacy and delicate. They giggled like they were playing dress up and changed into them. The girls brushed each other's hair and were soon a bridal party with a wedding to go to. As they started to leave the attic, it began to thunder and rain fell loudly on the roof.

Esther grabbed the leprechaunic button and slipped it

into her pocket. Until she figured out what to do with it, she didn't want it to fall into the wrong hands. As they rushed out of the attic, Father Herman and Connor were coming down from the roof to get out of the rain. The girls hid Fairleigh behind them and Connor shielded his eyes.

Bridget whispered to Esther, "I guess that old wives' tale about the groom not seeing the bride before the wedding is pretty ancient and also international!" The girls giggled and Father Herman kept making his way down the huge winding staircase. He called out, "Meet us in the parlor when you hear the piano playing!"

Soon piano music drifted through the castle halls, and holding the train of Fairleigh's dress, the girls made their way slowly down the grand staircase. Thunder crashed loudly outside and made it hard not to jump, it was so loud. The fireplaces were noisily crackling as the immense fires inside them glowed with comfort and warmth. The priest's butler was playing the piano and the cook was discreetly placing a beautiful spread of food out in the adjoining dining room.

Fairleigh walked slowly towards Connor. Bridget and Esther arranged the train and stood beside her. Caitlin and Kayla stood alongside Connor. The music permeated the loving atmosphere and Father Herman married them in a circle of stars that moved like tiny dancers swaying as they made a continuous circle of light around the couple.

Then the priest announced them husband and wife and asked Connor to kiss his bride. As Connor kissed Fairleigh, an identical crown of emeralds materialized on Fairleigh's beautiful red head. After Connor released her, he smiled. Fairleigh reached up to touch the crown and squealed with glee.

Father Herman shouted, "I knew something special would happen when I married the two of you! I now pronounce you husband and wife!" As he uttered those last words, two identical pure emerald bands of solid continuous precious stone materialized on their fingers. Rings like these had never been seen before. They were solid circles of emerald, no gold or diamonds, but they shone with power and beauty and were exquisite. Everyone gasped in astonishment at the magical gift, especially the bride and groom.

Then another magical thing happened: their ring hands, as though they were magnets and controlled like puppets, rose into the air, clinked like crystal, and stuck together. A quiet lightning bolt came from thin air, shot through the rings and parted into two bolts. One of the bolts went through Fairleigh and the other through Connor, encircling their bodies, then met again at the rings and became one bolt again and disappeared into thin air. Church bells rang loudly in the distance. Was it a coincidence? It was as though they were bound by the spirit of God, truly married and made into one. The couple glowed with happiness. This was a true bonding.

Esther grabbed Bridget's arm and whispered, "It's as though God blessed this marriage. They've got to be special soul mates!" Connor kissed his bride again and then they both hugged Father Herman. Music drifted romantically from the piano. The two began to dance and the Father ushered everyone into the dining room, whispering: "Let them have a quiet moment alone to dance."

"You sure are romantic for a priest," Bridget giggled. A magnificent feast was waiting. "Is it kosher?" Esther whispered to the cook.

"I knew we were meant for each other," Fairleigh whispered to Connor as they danced together for the first time as husband and wife.

"So did I," Connor held her close. "But now I know God knew it too."

"Girls, I hope you didn't mind the slight delay in hunting for the hope chest!" Connor smiled at the Americans.

"You must be joking! I wouldn't have missed this for the world," Bridget spoke with her mouth full of food.

Esther came back from the kitchen with a bewildered cook with a glass plate full of fruits and vegetables that she could eat. Apparently the cook didn't know what kosher meant. Esther had for certain been teaching her. They laughed as they caught the tail end of the conversation. Esther was explaining her Jewish dietary laws to a very interested but flustered cook.

"Now everybody please give me your attention." Father Herman rang a small bell at the end of the table, "This day isn't over yet. We have a plan. Caitlin and Kayla are going to summon the leprechauns. When they arrive, I plan to invite their leader inside. When we have him here I will tell him that they have a new princess, soon to be queen. When they see that they couldn't stop the wedding, I'm hoping they will accept Fairleigh."

"But Father," Bridget objected. "What if they don't accept her? What then? Will they try to hurt or even kill her?"

Father Herman gently took Bridget by the shoulders. "Don't fret, my dear, things will work out. If I can't reason with him, I'm going to undo the brainwashing. They can't go on like this forever. Let's all say some silent prayers while I tend to my preparations."

Father Herman went outside and everyone bowed their heads in a silent prayer. Esther finished hers and went to Connor and pressed the button into his hand. "Keep this safe, I think you may need it," Esther whispered into his ear.

Connor opened his hand and gasped in astonishment. "Where did you get this? Do you have any idea what this is and what it means?"

Fairleigh, who had been talking to Bridget, overheard his anxious voice and said, "What is it, Connor? Esther, what's wrong?"

Esther explained, "Fairleigh, I've given Connor the button you found on Father Herman's mother's wedding dress. Do you still have the one you found on your dress?"

"But of course," Fairleigh said, "with all that's happened I haven't had a chance to show it to Connor and ask him what this meant, although we all know it held me under a spell."

"Fairleigh, did you discover the button yourself?" Connor asked anxiously.

"Why, yes, of course, on the trip from America back home in the hope chest, in that foggy mist I was entrapped in," she answered.

"Fairleigh, let me see it." Connor was so nervous, he shook as he held the button Esther had given him in his open palm and waited for Fairleigh to retrieve the other one. Fairleigh reached deep into her pocket and pulled it out. She held it out in her open palm and showed it to Connor.

Bridget and Esther hovered over them and the whole table of wedding guests was quiet. He carefully turned them both upside down revealing the clear beveled glass bottoms. "You girls have no idea what this means. There is an old leprechaunic fable saying that for me to find a princess to match my wits and love is as rare as it is for two people to find two leprechaunic buttons and meet again."

Connor looked at Fairleigh wid-eyed and said, "This is our answer to peace with the leprechauns. This is our answer to their accepting you as my wife, my princess. When we push the two buttons together they will become one and all spells will be broken. Whether good or evil prevails will be up to my discretion and the leprechauns will obey me once again. The rebellion will be over. I can restore honesty, integrity, kindness, good music and laughter to the leprechauns" Connor smiled and slouched down in his chair, suddenly fatigued at the prospect that this horrible chase might be at a permanent end.

Chapter 15

Suddenly there was a terrific noise outside. Everyone ran to the great window to see what the commotion was about. Father Herman and Kayla and Caitlin were flailing about like a bunch of ruffians trying to convince the great green crowd to calm down and stay outside.

"Oh, Bridget," Esther whispered. "I'm having an instinct rush, the leps are not going to accept this. This won't be as easy as Father Herman thinks. We need to get out of here before we endanger Father Herman and all these people."

Bridget, as always, believed her best friend and pulled on Connor's sleeve. "Please, let's get out a back way while the leps are distracted. We have to find the hope chest and we have to protect you and Fairleigh "

There was a terrible crash, the moat gate had come tumbling down and the noise of the leps was deafening. They had charged into the castle. Connor grabbed Fairleigh and with Bridget and Esther following, ran through the kitchen and out a back door. They ran on, around a back drawbridge for the servants, and through the front of the castle. Father Herman was on his knees crying and praying. He was disheveled and looked as though he had been roughed up.

"Run," he said, "they are out of control. I'll be fine, go, quickly," he shouted and waved them on. The four quickly hugged him and ran as fast as they could.

Connor screamed, "I'll have to leave without Kayla and Caitlin, please Father, take care of them." The old priest nodded and waved them on. They ran and ran although they could feel the green heat descending upon them. They finally came upon a meadow that Fairleigh recognized. "This is it. This is the meadow. The chest is hidden here."

They split up and looked around wildly. Esther cried,

"They are on the hill coming down." Suddenly Bridget shouted, "I found it." They all raced over to the chest. Connor helped Bridget and Esther in and they all hugged each other goodbye.

"I can't believe this is happening." Bridget began to cry. "It's too fast. I don't want to leave you all like this..."

"Here, take the button," Connor pressed one of the buttons into Esther's hand and Fairleigh pressed the other one into Bridget's. "Press the glass ends together. It will break the spell and take you home."

"No," Bridget cried and tried to press the button back into Connor's hand. "Then you and Fairleigh won't be able to stop the dreadful turmoil between you and the leprechauns." Esther also tried to put the other button back into Fairleigh's hand.

"Esther, Bridget, because of you two I am here, home, back in Ireland and married to Connor, please, take the buttons," Fairleigh pleaded. The kindness from Connor and Fairleigh was astounding. Here they were in trouble, maybe their lives were at stake and they were more worried about the girls.

"Wait, the key," Bridget cried out, "I forgot the key will take us back!"

"But you don't know that it will work this time, Bridget, you and Esther need to get home to your families," Connor frantically looked behind him.

Esther pressed her button firmly into Connor's hand, "Let me try. Remember what you told me about faith and certainty, Connor? To believe in the letters and what's right? I believe. I believe the key and the letters will take us home!"

Bridget went to grab Fairleigh's hand to press the button into her hand as well when suddenly the forgotten chameleon jumped into the hope chest. He had grown attached to Esther and had followed them. When he jumped in the hope chest, the entire contents and the girls became invisible to the approaching leps. Little did the leps know that they were all there, just camouflaged.

Suddenly a large green leprechaun jumped up and

grabbed Fairleigh back by the hair. The button went flying in the air as Esther pulled Bridget into the chest.

Almost instantly little Kayla appeared, dove into the grass, grabbed the button and pushed it into Fairleigh's hand as Connor struggled to pull the leprechaun off of Fairleigh. Instinctively Fairleigh and Connor reached for each other's hands in the midst of the struggle and the buttons touched.

Colorful sparks flew everywhere; there was an explosion of light and the leprechaun was exploded off of Fairleigh into the meadow. The group was surrounded by leprechauns strangely frozen by the sight. Fairleigh and Connor held each other as a bubble of sparkly mist enclosed them in a protective white light. The leprechauns collapsed on their knees in the meadow; their heads bowed low in shame.

The nasty faces were gone, a softened look had returned to each leprechaun. Suddenly Timothy Klein popped out of the sky and landed on the soft grass. He was bound and gagged. He looked drugged. Connor knew then that the leprechauns had given his faithful servant some sort of brew. Connor's eyes shot arrows of light towards Timothy Klein. The arrows weaved in and out of the ropes, dissolving them. As they disappeared, the groggy older man servant came out of his drugged stupor. He rubbed his eyes and caught glance of his master.

Struggling to his feet with the help of that exquisite cane, he hobbled over to Connor. Bowing low to his prince, the elderly servant handed over the remarkable cane with emerald eyes that he held gently on open palms. Instantly the cane converted back into a staff! Connor took his father's staff with a smile and held it lovingly against his chest. This was the staff that would give him full power. Fairleigh, behind Connor, lay her head against his shoulder with arms around his waist.

"The spell is broken, Prince Connor. You reign now as King." Timothy Klein smiled back and brightly lit arrows bounced back and forth between the two.

Now it was time to get the Americans back home. Connor and Fairleigh went over to the hope chest and hugged the girls tightly.

Bridget, with tears streaming down her face sobbed, "Connor, Fairleigh, we don't know how to say goodbye, will we see each other again?"

"If you are certain then we will," Connor smiled and led the girls over to the hope chest and held their hands like ladies in waiting, up in the air, as they climbed in. He kissed each girl's hand and bowed as he backed away from the hope chest. Fairleigh hugged them and kissed them on each cheek, just like those Europeans do!

With tears in their eyes, Bridget and Esther crouched down. The chameleon jumped in behind them and scurried under Esther's skirt unnoticed. The girls shut the lid of the chest and turned the key in the lock together. The hope chest vanished but the girls were certain they would see their Irish friends again.

Final Chapter

Back in Bridget's bedroom, Natalie looked aghast as the chest rematerialized – it had been gone only a few seconds. Bridget and Esther opened the lid and began to climb out.

"Where were you guys?" Natalie gripped the arms of the club chair she was still trying to weigh down with all of her 80 pounds. Bridget's mom was angrily yelling from the other side of the door.

"Natalie, you can't believe what happened to us," both girls started talking at once, "but first let's let my mom in or she'll kill me."

The girls moved the club chair out of the way. After they opened the door, Bridget grabbed Esther's hand with both of hers and coincidentally when she did so, Esther didn't realize it but the copper belt around her skirt suddenly changed to the color of her skirt and glowed mysteriously. At the same time Bridget's little birthstone ring that she always wore turned the color of her skin. Bridget also didn't notice. The chameleon, hidden amongst the folds of Esther's skirt and camouflaged in the same colors, slid out unnoticed and into the closet.

Bridget's mom stood with hands on her hips.

"What took you so long to open the door and what are you girls up to? What has happened to the chest?" She turned to Mr. Klein who had suddenly disappeared and the girls turned around to what was now a vanished chest. The girls shrugged their shoulders at a very confused mom and the chameleon in the closet winked his eye as stars encircled his little body.

THE END

About the Illustrator

Tess Heimbach grew up in a Roman Catholic military family and has lived all over the world. She is a Jill-of-all-Trades and now lives in San Diego, California, with her son. Her degrees are in Sculpture, Painting & Printmaking, and Art History at SDSU Primarily working on a large scale in oils, she also enjoys working with watercolors, pencil, wood, bronze, graphic design, and mixed media. Her work conveys the artist's process, thereby providing her audience with a method by which to personally connect with her imagery. For more information about Tess, please visit her website at www.artesstry.com.

Melanie Ross, the author of The Hope Chest can be contacted through Underwood Publishing at 7290 Navajo Road Suite 110, San Diego, Ca 92119.
UnderwoodPublishing.com
E-Mail: Melanie@UnderwoodPublishing.com
(See back cover for Melanie's story)